James Philip

The Big City

UNTIL THE NIGHT – BOOK THREE

Copyright © James P. Coldham writing as James Philip, in respect of The Big City, Book 3 of the Until the Night Series (the serialisation of the 2nd Edition of Until the Night), 2015. All rights reserved.

Cover concept by James Philip
Graphic Design by Beastleigh Web Design

The Bomber War Series

Book 1: Until the Night
Book 2: The Painter
Book 3: The Cloud Walkers

Until the Night Series

A serialisation of Book 1: Until the Night in five parts

Part 1: Main Force Country – September 1943
Part 2: The Road to Berlin – October 1943
Part 3: The Big City – November 1943
Part 4: When Winter Comes – December 1943
Part 5: After Midnight – January 1944

The Big City

We can wreck Berlin from end to end if the USAAF come in with us. It will cost us between 400 and 500 aircraft. It will cost Germany the war.

Victory, speedy and complete, awaits the side which first employs air power as it should be employed. Germany, entangled in the meshes of vast land campaigns, cannot now disengage her air power for a strategically proper application. She missed victory through air power by a hair's breadth in 1940... We ourselves are now at the crossroads.

Air Marshall Sir Arthur Harris
[Air Officer Commanding-in-Chief RAF Bomber Command]

Chapter 1

Sunday 6th November, 1943
RAF Grafton Priory, Shrewsbury, Shropshire

Suzy stifled a yawn as she packed her kit. The other women on the course watched her idly, some with veiled sympathy, most with indifference. Everybody was tired, fed up. About a dozen girls from the other huts had been singled out, ordered to prepare to transfer off the course but only Suzy from among the women in hut No. 11.

Flight Sergeant Richards, their drill instructor had marched into the hut at mid-day, glanced at his clipboard and bawled out: "ACW Mills to report to the Senior WAAF at fifteen-thirty hours! Take your kit with you!" And stomped out without another word.

Suzy was very nearly beyond caring. She had come down with a head cold the day she left Ansham Wolds and not been able to shake it off. Every morning they drilled on the big, windswept parade ground, in the afternoons there were aptitude tests, medical examinations, endless sessions cleaning and packing kit, inspections and practice alarms. She had been at Grafton Priory less than a week but it felt like a month.

RAF Grafton Priory was a big, ivy-infested mansion a couple of miles outside Shrewsbury. The Priory itself was used for classrooms and accommodated the mess hall. WAAFs under training lived in the rows of numbered Nissen huts in the woods behind the big house. At any one time several courses were in progress. Each day began before dawn and candidates were hustled, bustled, intimidated, chased and generally harried from then until lights out at nine o'clock in the evening. Nobody was allowed off the base and everybody was under the microscope, everybody was on trial every single minute. It was a trial that Suzy suspected she had already failed. Failed almost before it had begun. She had struggled from the outset, partly because of her head cold, partly because many of the other girls were physically bigger and stronger than she was, but mostly she struggled because she desperately missed Peter. She missed him so much she could have cried herself to sleep at night. What made it infinitely worse was that she felt horribly guilty, as if she had deserted him and somehow, left him to his fate.

Everything had gone wrong. If she failed the course they would send her straight back to 1 Group for reassignment. She could be sent anywhere in quasi disgrace. How could she face Peter? She would have cried her eyes out that afternoon had she not been so determined *not* to show weakness in front of the others.

To make matters worse she had yet to receive a letter from Peter. He had warned her letters took an age to catch up; even so, she yearned to hear from him. For any sign that she was not alone in this dreadful place.

The Senior WAAF was a tall, slim woman in her thirties. Suzy stood before her, swaying. Dragging her kit bag across the parade ground in the rain had exhausted what little remained of her dwindling strength. Her face was flushed. She sniffed and could not prevent herself sneezing.

"At ease, Mills," directed the older woman, viewing her thoughtfully. "And for goodness sake blow your nose!"

"Yes, ma'am." Suzy did as she was instructed.

"I've reviewed your file." The Senior WAAF paused, sighed. "I see that you were the Station Master's driver at Ansham Wolds?"

"Yes, ma'am," Suzy replied, and blew her nose.

"For three? No, four months?"

"Yes, ma'am." To Suzy's surprise, not to say her mild consternation, the Senior WAAF suddenly smiled a wry, unexpectedly kindly smile.

"I should imagine you know more about what's going on over Germany than practically anybody here at Grafton Priory?"

"I wouldn't say that, ma'am," Suzy ventured, uncomfortably.

"No? You'd be surprised, Mills. Group Captain Alexander says you're an extremely bright girl with lots of initiative. I've seen enough this week to confirm his view. That's why I've decided to withdraw you from your present course and post you directly onto the Ops Course."

"Oh, I see..."

"You don't sound very enthusiastic, Mills?"

"No, it's not that, Ma'am," Suzy explained, nervously. "It's just that when I was ordered to report to you I was afraid I was going to be send back to Group, that's all."

The Senior WAAF shook her head. The first cull of dullards was reserved for the second Monday of each course. By then, the better officer candidates, like ACW Mills, had been quietly winnowed from the herd.

"Work hard in the next few weeks," she advised the younger woman, "and you'll be returning to Group with your commission. I probably shouldn't tell you this, but you're exactly the sort of material the Ops people like to work with. Off you go, now. Report to Hut Twenty. And, Mills! First thing tomorrow morning make sure you report to the flight surgeon. See if he can't give you some powders for that cold of yours!"

"Yes, ma'am."

Chapter 2

Thursday 18th November, 1943
RAF Ansham Wolds, Lincolnshire

"FIGHTER STARBOARD!" Taffy screamed. "CORKSCREW PORT. NOW! NOW! NOW! HE'S FOLLOWING US DOWN! CORKSCREW STARBOARD! NOW! NOW! NOW..."

Adam awoke in a cold sweat.

It was pitch black in his quarters. Beads of perspiration trickled down his brow although the air was bitterly cold. His breath misted in his face as he took a series of long, slow breaths to calm his inner demons. His cot was a shambles, the sheets strewn about him and on the floor.

"God..."

Presently, his pulse slowed, the blind terror subsided. He involuntarily reached for his cigarette case on the small table by the head of the bed. His hands shook when he struck a match.

The dreams were getting worse. Much worse.

It was nearly a month since he had flown an op, the Kassel show. In the intervening weeks the Squadron had operated on just one night, participating in the Main Force attack on Dusseldorf. That was a fortnight ago. Since then 1 Group's Lancasters had missed out on milk runs to the marshalling yards at Modane and Cannes, and sat out last night's trip to Mannheim-Ludwigshafen. That apparently, had been a wholly 8 Group affair. Some sort of a trial, an experimental show of some kind.

He smoked his cigarette, waited for his equilibrium to return.

It was a little after six o'clock. Swinging his long legs over the side of the cot, he got to his feet. Washing and shaving in icy water, he donned his battledress. Rufus remained curled up in his basket, viewing his master with sleepily attentive eyes.

"Walkies!"

Outside it was still dark. The clouds were high and overnight the wind had dropped to a whisper. A frost lay hard and crisp on the ground.

There would be a major attack tonight. The old Moon had waned two nights ago and now that the weather had broken the Chief would surely hurl the Main Force at the Big City.

Tonight.

The day of reckoning had arrived.

Berlin was six hundred miles from England, the third largest city in the world with a pre-war population of over four million and a metropolitan area of some 883 square miles. The city had grown up on the sandy flood plain of the River Spree and contained within its boundaries vast tracts of park and woodland, and countless lakes and canals. Wide open spaces - stretches of water and forest – completely fragmented the urban landscape. Unlike London or Hamburg, Berlin was a modern city: a city of concrete apartment blocks, and well-founded, sturdy buildings likely to withstand anything but a direct hit. Berlin had no old, wooden heart. No *Altstadt.* Problematically, the streets of the city were broad and straight; superb natural firebreaks.

The Main Force had already gone to Berlin eight times in 1943, despatching over three thousand heavy bomber sorties. A combination of bad weather, the inability of the Pathfinders to find and mark the aiming point and the unparalleled ferocity of the Berlin flak had to date, hamstrung Bomber Command. Some bombs had fallen on the German capital's southern, mainly residential districts, but the central area, wherein lay the great state buildings and the administrative hub of the Third Reich, and the northern, heavily industrialised quarters of Berlin remained after four years of war, virtually unscathed. While no part of London was without its seas of ruins, Berlin remained the city it had been before the war, scarcely violated by high explosives and fire.

The pre-dawn twilight touched the eastern horizon.

Six hundred miles east of Ansham Wolds the dawn had already broken over Berlin.

Chapter 3

Thursday 18th November, 1943
St. Paul's Church, Ansham Wolds, Lincolnshire

Eleanor heard the first Merlins revving up in the distance. A few minutes later a Lancaster thundered over the square Norman tower of St. Paul's Church. The village children went on playing in the yard outside, oblivious to the Lancasters taking off and climbing high above Ansham Wolds. The sky was clear and the sun shone brightly that winter's morning as she watched and listened to the bombers circling the aerodrome.

Flight tests. All aircraft had to be flight tested before the crews were briefed. She had extracted this much, if little else, from Adam. Raids were often called off later in the day, she reminded herself. She might yet see her dashing Wing-Commander that evening. They had settled into a routine of a kind. He had turned up on her doorstep unannounced a couple of times but Thursday evenings had become a fixture in their diaries. It was the one time each week when they would arrange to be together and alone at the cottage. It was all very innocent. She would feed him, they would talk, laugh, cuddle, kiss in the dark before the fire. Then he would run back to her rival: his precious Squadron and his beloved Lancasters. She begrudged him neither. How could she? It was 647 Squadron and the Lancasters that had brought him to Ansham Wolds in the first place.

Adam joined her for Evensong on Sunday when he could. Occasionally, he would turn up unannounced at the Church Hall around lunch time. Just to say "hello". One Saturday he had brought Ben Hardiman to the cottage, they had shared several pots of tea, and reminisced about Boscombe Down, her brother David and their Kelmington days on 380 Squadron. Ben was such a nice man, there was no side to him. In that way at least, her beau's navigator reminded her a little of her dead husband. There the similarity ended. Ben Hardiman was altogether more Devil may care than Harry...

A Lancaster flew over the Church.

So low it almost brushed the parapet.

It banked into a tight, anti-clockwise turn and droned back up the valley, levelling out somewhere beyond the village. Then the bomber returned. She heard it coming long before she saw it. When it flew into sight it was very low, down in the valley at the same elevation as the Church Hall. So low that its wing tips seemed to be skimming through the treetops. So low she could see into the cockpit. So low she could not drag her eyes away from the bomber. Eleanor had never seen a Lancaster flying so low, or so near that she felt as if she could almost reach out and touch it.

The note of its engines suddenly changed, slowing to a deep, rumbling growl that reverberated across the wold. As it drew abreast the Church she saw arms raised in the big, long cockpit and by the men in the mid-upper and rear turrets. Arms raised and waving as the sun glinted on the polished Perspex. She read the big red identification numbers on the fuselage, mouthing the letters silently to herself. The Squadron code PC to the left of the RAF roundel, O to the right, identifying the aircraft as O for Orange. She saw the faces of the gunners in their turrets, the fixed tail-wheel spinning slowly in the slipstream between the tall twin tail flukes.

The pilot waggled the Lancaster's wings as he flew out of the valley. The pitch of Merlin engines quickened and the bomber climbed steeply into the bright blue of the November morning. Eleanor's son, Jonathan had gravitated to her side. He stared up at the bomber with undiluted awe and she was no less moved.

"Is that Uncle Adam's aeroplane, Mummy?" The boy asked.

For a moment she said nothing, distracted.

"Yes, dear."

Chapter 4

Thursday 18th November, 1943
RAF Ansham Wolds, Lincolnshire

Peter Tilliard returned to his quarters after the main crew briefing. There were two hours to kill before the off and it would be at least an hour before the Bedford lorry collected them for the ride out to the dispersals.

Jack Gordon followed him into the room.

"Oh well," he announced, stretching out on his cot. "Big City here we come! Don't forget to wake me up before the off." This said, he pulled his cap over his face, placed his hands behind his head and concentrated on the serious business of catching up on his sleep.

Tilliard smiled to himself, shook his head.

Jack was one of the oddest chaps he had ever known. Notwithstanding, they had become the firmest of friends.

After the Hanover raid they had both found themselves minus their old roommates.

'For Christ's sake! Move your kit in quick,' Jack had exhorted him. 'Before they unload some snotty-nosed little sprog on me!' Tilliard had needed no second invitation. He had swiftly moved into the Australian's billet.

That was four weeks ago: a lifetime on the squadrons.

Since then Tilliard had reached a personal milestone: the Dusseldorf op being the tenth of his second tour. Notwithstanding, that two of those ten ops had been early returns - early returns without bombing a target in Germany did not count towards the magic figure of twenty which constituted a completed *second* tour - nobody in the *Hare and Hounds* in Kingston Magna the next night cared a hoot. Given 647 Squadron's recent grisly history, surviving ten ops was a thing to celebrate. Even Barney Knight had looked in, albeit fleetingly, making a point of very publicly buying a round of drinks and equally publicly, heartily slapping him on the back before departing for the fleshpots of Lincoln.

Tilliard pulled up the chair at the rickety table at the foot of his cot.

He wrote to Suzy every day, ops or no ops, and this was the first opportunity he had had to sit down with pen and paper today.

Dearest Suzy,

Not long to go, now. Op number eleven coming up and it's the big one at last. Berlin. Lancaster Force at maximum effort to the Big City; Halifaxes and Stirlings to Ludwigshafen. (Yes, I know I'm not supposed to name names - the censor chappie can scratch the names out if he wants! It's not as if it won't all be in the papers tomorrow, anyway).

We're "off" early today: 17:10.

Jack's having a snooze, as usual. I don't know how the blighter does it! Me, I'm a bag of nerves right up until the "off". It's odd, that. Once we're on our way all the butterflies in the tummy literally fly away.

The latest talk is that the Squadron will be expanded into a three-flight formation. It may just be gossip but it would make a lot of sense. Either that or they might move in another Squadron. We shall see what transpires in due course, I suppose.

It has been a beautiful day today. Clear skies, plenty of sunshine – it is supposed to be cloudy and rainy over Germany, of course!

I got your letter of the 10th this morning. You don't know how relieved I am to hear that you're making friends and that the Ops Course is now going so swimmingly. You sounded so lonely and unhappy in your earlier letters that I was tempted to steal a kite and fly down there to rescue you. (That's not to say I wouldn't still do just that if you asked me!).

I spoke to the Wingco today about the Conversion Flight. I reminded him that the original idea was to rotate all the old lags through it - and that, with respect, I seemed to have got well and truly "lumbered". He was kind enough to say I was doing such a good job he didn't like to put our sprogs in anybody else's hands. (A lot of old flannel, I know). I said I was quite happy to carry on, if that was what he wanted me to do. It's very hard to say "no" to the Wingco. Not that I'd particularly want to say "no" if you see what I mean. None of us want to let him down. Even Barney's old lags are coming round. As for my sprogs; to a man they are in absolute awe of the Wingco. Anyway, back to the Conversion Flight. The Wingco was chatting away, all business as usual, no messing about, when he looked me in the eye and he said something like: "The thing is, Peter, whatever happens you've got to try to keep thinking ahead. What are the possibilities?" Or words to that effect.

I'm blowed if I know what it was all about but the Wingco usually knows what he's talking about.

What else has happened? Oh, yes. Did I mention that I've now acquired a couple of "regular" gunners (finally)? Good, solid types. Old lags. Lucky to get them, really. Jack knew one fellow, Dave, our new tail-end charlie from his first tour. The other chap, Fred, used to be an instructor at 31 OTU, and was doing his level best to avoid having to fly with sprogs. When I asked him if he wanted to fly with us he almost hugged me. It was a tad embarrassing, to be honest. Still, as I say they are both fine chaps and I feel much happier now I've got a settled crew.

Anyway, you're half way through your course now. I can't wait to see you again. Please don't worry about me, I shall be fine. It's silly, I know. But I feel that whatever happens, we shall come through, if you know what I mean.

All my love.
Peter

Tilliard put down his pen.
There was so much he wanted to say to Suzy.

He thought about her all the time, it seemed the most natural thing in the world. Life was good. Life had meaning, life was precious. He was utterly besotted with a beautiful girl and she loved him, too. But Suzy was in Shrewsbury and for the next few hours he had to put her out of his mind and focus on tonight's entertainment.

His life and the lives of the men he was flying with depended upon it.

Jack Gordon was snoring loudly on his cot and time was ticking by.

Tilliard glanced at his watch.

He folded the pages, slipped them into the envelope, scrawled the address, sealed the flap. He left the letter on the table, he would post it tomorrow.

When he got back.

The Wingco was right. The way to survive was by believing that there was always a tomorrow. And that there were always possibilities.

He shook Jack's shoulder.

The Australian stirred.

"Show time, old man," Tilliard said quietly.

Chapter 5

Thursday 18th November, 1943
Lancaster O-Orange, 40 miles West of Texel

Ben Hardiman checked the star sights against his *Gee* fixes. Satisfied, he flicked his intercom switch.

"Navigator to pilot." The intercom hissed, the Merlins droned, fingers of frost bit deep into his bones.

"Pilot to navigator. Are we on track, Ben?"

"On the nail, Skipper. Concentration point in three minutes. Our altitude should read twelve thousand five hundred feet, over."

"Altimeter shows eleven thousand feet."

"Navigator to pilot. The dial shows eleven thousand feet. Out."

O-Orange was straining for height over the North Sea. Tonight, more than any other night it was essential to fly on track and as close as possible to the specified altitudes all the way to the target. Normally, the Main Force bombed within a thirty to forty minute window. Tonight, the Lancaster Force operating at maximum effort - over 400 aircraft - was tasked to bomb between 20:56 and 21:12. By drastically shortening the duration of the attack it was hoped to frustrate the fighters and lessen the killing power of the Berlin flak.

Ben was sceptical. Shortening the duration of the attack increased both the collision risk and the likelihood of being bombed by other heavies. Moreover, because a large number of Lancasters - all of 1 Group's aircraft - were over-loaded it was unlikely that the bomber stream would form properly until it was deep inside Germany, if at all. In any case, there was no way around the Berlin flak. You had to see the Berlin flak to believe it. There was nothing on earth quite like the Berlin flak!

Well, nothing this side of Hades, leastways.

"Navigator to pilot. Concentration point NOW. Turn starboard onto one-oh-oh degrees." Up ahead the Pathfinders would be crossing the enemy coast a few miles north of Den Helder, pushing on over the Zuider Zee. Two hundred and fifty miles southwest a second force of around 400 heavies – made up of every available Halifax and Stirling and about 30 Lancasters - would be over Abbeville, heading for Ludwigshafen. Never before had Bomber Command mounted two such massive simultaneous attacks on separate targets in Germany. Ben prayed silently, guiltily, that tonight the fighters would be sent to the south.

The Lancaster Force was flying a direct route to the Big City: across Holland passing Groningen to port, into Germany south of Oldenburg, thence into Saxony keeping north of the line Hanover - Brunswick - Magdeburg, and onto Brandenburg where the blind markers would hope against hope to get a firm *H2S* fix prior to commencing their final timed bombing run. Tonight, there were no doglegs, no feints. Nothing to confuse sprog navigators.

"Thinking bad, doing good," Ben muttered to himself. There would be time enough to get twitchy another night. He went up to the astrodome at the rear of the cockpit, tried to get a couple more star sights. O-Orange's *H2S* set had started smoking immediately after takeoff so he had switched it off. The set might have allowed him to fix their landfall over Texel, but otherwise, he was not unduly concerned to have to make do without the infernal device because the weather was forecast to be clear most of the way to Berlin.

Aircrew lore: *St Sod* was the patron saint of Bomber Command.

In the event the weather forecast was wrong. Over Holland O-Orange climbed into layer upon layer of thick, impenetrable cloud.

Clouds which enveloped, blinded and shielded the Main Force.

Chapter 6

Thursday 18th November, 1943
Lancaster T-Tommy, 20 miles NNE of Brunswick

T-Tommy eventually climbed out of the cloud a hundred miles inside Germany. Having navigated half-way across northern Europe by dead reckoning and guesswork, Jack Gordon allowed himself a heartfelt sigh of relief as the stars came out. His relief however, was short-lived. The sky was full of heavies, above, below and to either side. Everywhere he looked, in fact.

"Rear Gunner to pilot," called Dave Wrigley, the short, wiry Ulsterman Jack knew from his first tour. "I recommend we give the weaving a rest, Skipper. There's kites all over the shop back here."

"Pilot to rear gunner. Roger, out." Peter Tilliard acknowledged. The aircraft steadied on track.

Jack Gordon set about getting a much needed star sight. Back in his cluttered cubby hole he checked and re-checked T-Tommy's position.

"Navigator to pilot. We're about five miles north of the planned ground track, Skipper. The forecast winds must be wrong."

There was a short delay before Tilliard responded.

"Thanks, Jack. We'll stay on this heading and cut the corner north of Brandenburg. We seem to be nicely tucked into the stream. No point going out on a limb. Over."

"Navigator to pilot. Understood."

Jack started to calculate how far T-Tommy had

to run before the next turn. That turn, north-east of Brandenburg, would aim the Lancaster's nose, in theory, directly at the aiming point situated in the middle of the giant *Siemensstadt* industrial complex in the north-west quarter of Berlin. T-Tommy rocked and shuddered as she flew through disturbed air churned by the passage of scores of other heavies.

Up ahead the sky was on fire. The Brandenburg flak had opened up. Brandenburg, thirty miles short of the AP marked the outermost circle of the Big City's flak defences. The first line of defence. There seemed no way through the barrage. Normally, flak was co-ordinated with the fighters, each had their own bit of the sky. Tonight, the gunners were firing without restriction, filling the night with a seemingly impenetrable wall of shot and shell.

"Pilot to bomb-aimer."

"Bomb-aimer to pilot, over." Reported Billy Campbell, the twenty-year-old Glaswegian baby of the crew. Campbell was a friend of the Wingco's bomb-aimer, Round Again, who had recommended him to Tilliard before the Dusseldorf op at the beginning of the month. Billy was new to ops, this being only his fourth trip. Apart from having to throw *Window* out of the aircraft at regular intervals which was cold, boring work, he still thought ops were a breeze.

"You can stop *Windowing*, Billy," Tilliard told him, evenly, almost gagging on the words. His mouth and throat had gone dry. "I think the opposition know we're coming, now. Get down to the nose and check your equipment."

T-Tommy droned on towards the curtain of fire hanging high above Brandenburg. The black silhouettes of countless Lancasters drifted into the east like a swarm of dark, avenging angels while searchlights played across the bottom of the clouds a mile below. In the distance the openers shouldered through the flak, searching for the illusory sanctuary of the open skies beyond.

However, there was no sanctuary beyond Brandenburg. Only more gun lines, more and heavier calibre guns.

"Jesus... Are we supposed to fly through that!" Whistled Billy Campbell, lying on top of the escape hatch in the nose, gazing with mounting horror at the Brandenburg flak.

Tilliard flicked his intercom switch. "Pilot to bomb-aimer. Be a good fellow and keep off the circuit unless you've got something to report, Billy!"

"Bomb-aimer to pilot. Sorry, Skipper. Bomb-aimer in position. Over."

The Lancaster pitched into the flak. Shrapnel peppered the leading edges of her wings, blast waves tipped her this way and that. It was the first time Tilliard had actually *heard* the flak. Bulldozing on through the thunder flashes and the shrapnel was standard drill, *hearing* the detonations was not. T-Tommy roared into clean, unsullied skies. All was quiet but for the reassuring bellow of the Merlins. A moment later at two o'clock high a huge box of thin air – hundreds of feet square - was rent by a salvo of shells. Where previously there had been a pure, inky blackness, a split second later there was a crimson hell, a storm of red hot metal, chaos and death. Tilliard swallowed hard. Anything flying in the vicinity of the maelstrom would have simply ceased to exist.

The Big City was somewhere under the clouds. In the south was Potsdam. Beyond Potsdam a bright yellow route-marker was falling slowly into the outer residential districts of Berlin.

"Bomb-aimer to pilot," came the urgent, shaken voice of the young Scot in the nose. "I can't make out any ground features, Skipper. What do you want me to do?"

"Pilot to bomb-aimer. Keep looking, Billy."

While the forecast had not discounted the possibility of cloud over the target, nobody in England had predicted ten-tenths over the entire city. Consequently, the crews had been briefed to bomb on green target indicators. Green TIs and no others. Tilliard knew each Pathfinder carried, as a matter of standard procedure, at least one Sky Marker in its bomb bay. The question was: would the Pathfinders modify the marking scheme as the attack progressed? Drop Sky Markers as well as green TIs? He suspected not. That would be hoping for too much. He decided to wait a little longer before he told Billy what was what. In the meantime he would find out what Jack had to say on the subject.

"Pilot to navigator. It looks like we've got ten-tenths over the target up to about twelve thousand feet. There are green TIs going down at six o'clock, range approximately five miles. Another group is going down at four o'clock, range seven to eight miles. No Sky Markers yet, over."

Jack Gordon looked at his chart. "Navigator to pilot. The TIs may be short," he reported. "Unless we get a Sky Marker to bomb I recommend we bomb beyond the southern group, over."

Two miles below hundreds of searchlights blazed onto the underside of the clouds. Flak bursting in tight, killing boxes roamed the skies. Up in the north a streamer of flame signified the death of a heavy.

Where were the fighters?

Tilliard and every other man over Berlin was asking himself exactly the same question. Green TIs were burning all across the city, now. They fell in a dozen scattered groups, sparkling, dripping iridescent emerald fire, glowing briefly, unnaturally before they disappeared into the clouds, snuffed out in a moment. The clouds boiled as cookies struck ground. In the near distance hundreds and hundreds of incendiaries spilled from the gaping belly of another Lancaster.

"Pilot to bomb-aimer," Tilliard decided. "Bomb one mile beyond on the TIs directly ahead."

The bomb bay doors opened into the slipstream, stiffening the controls, slowing the aircraft. One or two terse requests to execute minor course changes followed, then T-Tommy reared upwards, relieved of her four-ton bomb load.

There was still no sign of night fighters as T-Tommy raced into a shallow dive, throttles wide open. Remarkably, for all the fury of the flak Tilliard had still only seen one heavy go down. The words 'bloodbath' and 'Berlin' were supposed to be synonymous. Things appeared to have worked out otherwise, tonight.

Chapter 7

Thursday 18th November, 1943
Lancaster O-Orange, 5 miles South of Werneuchen

O-Orange flew away from Berlin shaken, stirred but otherwise intact. The ferocity of the flak had come as a rude shock even to her old lags. Round Again had bombed the most northerly of the numerous green TIs on offer.

Twenty miles east of the city the Main Force swung due south, and began the long haul back to England into the teeth of the west wind. Ahead lay a four to five hour flight south-west across Germany between Leipzig and Kassel, then westward, through the Frankfurt - Cologne gap, on over the Ardennes, Picardy and the Channel making landfall at Selsey Bill on the south coast of England in the small hours of the morning. Over Lincolnshire the returning crews would probably have to stooge about in the stack over Ansham Wolds for at least another hour. O-Orange would have been in the air for around ten hours by the time she landed.

In O-Orange's rear turret Taffy Davies stared into the night. The cold was fierce, unrelenting. His neck ached and he could hardly feel his hands or his feet but he never stopped scanning the sky for danger, swinging the quadruple Fraser Nash type-20 turret from beam to beam. He tried not to peer overlong into the darkness because if you did you tended to lose perspective. It was better to look hard briefly, move your head, look again.

Periodically, he checked the breech blocks of his four 0.303-inch Browning machine guns.

One night in March, coming back from Duisburg he had dozed off momentarily and come around as a night fighter, a big ugly Messerschmitt, slid in on his tail and lined up to open fire at point blank range. He had screamed a despairing warning over the intercom:

"FIGHTER PORT! CORKSCREW STARBOARD! NOW!"

Attempted, to all intents posthumously, to bring his guns to bear. Nothing had happened. Absolutely nothing. The aircraft had flown on serenely - the intercom was broken - and his guns had remained silent with the blunt grey nose of the Me110 literally filling his sights. His Brownings had frozen solid. He had waited. Waited and waited, staring down the barrels of the Messerschmitt's cannons for what had seemed like an eternity, bracing himself for the end. He had known that he was about to die and resigned himself to it. Then, inexplicably, the fighter had broken away to be instantly lost in the night.

The mid-upper gunner had seen nothing: he was a dozy bastard. The rest of the crew thought he had imagined it – or dozed off and dreamed the whole thing - and he had never told anybody else about the incident. That was the last time he flew with sprogs. Never again, he had resolved.

He peered out into the nothingness. The Skipper was calling around the crew stations. He called around every few minutes, without fail. Taffy had flown with pilots who never exchanged a word with their gunners from take off to landing. Dead pilots. All dead now. Dead like the sprogs he had gone to Duisburg with in March.

"Pilot to rear gunner, talk to me please!"

Taffy grinned to himself. The Skipper wanted more than a routine acknowledgement, he wanted a man to sit up and take notice. In the intense cold it was far too easy to drift off into a state of half-consciousness, half-asleep, half-awake in which a man would shout out a simple: "Okay, Skipper!" And nod straight off to sleep, again. But not with the Wingco. The Wingco was a professional. He always made sure you were on the ball.

"Rear gunner to pilot. It's bloody cold back here, Skipper!"

"I'm sure it is, Taffy! You'll have to hang on a bit longer. Bert will be back with coffee when we've turned onto the next leg. Out!"

Taffy had not stopped searching the skies.

The W/T. operator, Bert Pound, took turns with Round Again to act as coffee monitor. On all but the coldest nights Taffy preferred caffeine pills, drinking coffee made him want to urinate every half-an-hour which was a disaster when there was 30 degrees of frost in the turret. On a night like this however, a man was a fool to refuse a warm drink. Even if it meant later having to piss into a bottle in 30 degrees of frost. He rotated the turret to port. Frostbitten privates were another thing they forgot to tell you about at the gunnery school. There were *a lot* of things they forgot to tell you about at gunnery school.

Bastards!

Taffy stiffened, thought he saw something moving: seven o'clock low. He blinked, screwed up his eyes, moved his head, peered hard. Nothing. He squinted into the blackness. There it was again.

Taffy relaxed.

It was another Lanc flying about two thousand feet below them. The turret whirred as it swung around, ammunition chains clinking dully at the end of each traverse. Heavy, clanking chains of bullets hung down from the breech of each gun, feeding back out of the base of the turret into ducts and boxes in the rear fuselage: 600 rounds per gun in each duct, a further 400 rounds per gun coiled and ready in the big feed boxes. In the old days they used to carry as much ammunition as they could cram into the boxes - 900 rounds per barrel - but some bright spark at Group had decided the weight could be put to better use carrying another couple of dozen incendiaries.

Bastards!

Taffy adjusted his face mask, painfully. The flight surgeon had wanted to knock him out and mess about resetting his nose. His nose had been giving him grief ever since three of B Flight's finest had worked him over outside *The Liberty* that night in Scunthorpe. He had told the medicos he was fine. The last thing he wanted was to be laid up in hospital and risk getting left behind again.

He made out the shapes of several other Lancasters against the background of the stars. Taffy started to hum a tune, shrugged in his electrically heated flying suit, stretched his limbs, left leg, right leg, right arm, left arm, rolled his head to ease the pains stabbing the back of his neck. Stay awake: keep looking, looking, looking.

Stay awake! Stay awake!

Scunthorpe tomorrow night, he promised himself.

He had scores to settle in Scunthorpe.

His eyes ceaselessly quartered the darkness behind O-Orange.

Where had all the fighters gone?

Chapter 8

Friday 19th November, 1943
RAF Ansham Wolds, Lincolnshire

The fighters had gone to Mannheim: 23 heavies had failed to return from the southern raid and the initial indications were that nearly all the casualties had fallen to night fighters. Confounding all expectations, only 9 Lancasters from the Berlin Force were missing. However, not everything in the garden was rosy.

Although Group Captain Alexander favoured putting the most optimistic possible gloss on the reports of the returning crews, even he was hard-pressed to claim any sort of success. Both Berlin and the twin city of Mannheim-Ludwigshafen had been cloud-covered. The Pathfinders' initial blind marking over both targets had been wide of the mark and scattered, as was the subsequent bombing effort.

"Absolute bloody shambles, sir," Adam confided, albeit well out of the hearing of any of his crews. "Nine to ten-tenths cloud over the target and the Pathfinders stuck to their original visual ground-marking plan!" It was pointless dropping TIs into the undercast. He had watched the concentrations of green TIs burning, sparkling, flashing in the night swallowed in the clouds over the Big City with something akin to despair. "Shambles!"

Barney Knight was holding forth at a nearby debriefing table.

"Flak? I should say, old chap," he informed the

Intelligence Officer. "Pretty fierce! Wouldn't have liked to have had to put my hand out of the window. What!" His crew chortled in unison, as did the pretty WAAF taking shorthand notes. The Intelligence Officer, a dour, humourless recent arrival at Ansham Wolds frowned uncomprehendingly as the younger man continued. "Flak, I'll say! It was so thick I could have walked home on it, old man! Now that's what I call proper flak!"

When the Squadron was stood down from operations later that morning Adam and the Station Master went for a walk. They often found themselves strolling together, out of earshot, exchanging confidences.

"You've got to stop pushing yourself so hard," Group Captain Alexander said, placing a heavy, paternal arm on Adam's shoulder. "This is only the beginning. You sit out a few ops. Rest up a bit."

Adam recognised that the advice was well-intentioned. Nevertheless, it rankled. He said nothing as they walked past the hangars.

"When was the last time you actually took any leave, by the way?" Demanded the Old Man, cloaking his concern with a mask of jocularity.

"June, sir."

"There you are! High time you took some more!"

"Yes, sir," Adam concurred, lowly, sulkily. "I shall give the matter some thought."

"Make sure you do."

They strolled on, diverting briefly to inspect the flak marks on Y-Yorker. A shard of white hot metal the size of a man's fist had entered the fuselage just forward the rear turret, demolished the Elsan chemical toilet, ricocheted off the ammunition ducts, severed the power and hydraulics lines to the turret and lodged in the stinking spillage from the Elsan between the starboard ammunition boxes. The rear turret, traversed hard over to port had jammed, trapping the unfortunate, nineteen year old gunner. Despite frantic efforts, other members of the crew had been unable to free him. Without voltage to heat his flying suit and with the slipstream ripping mercilessly through the turret, the five hour flight back to England had been a nightmare. The boy, a Czech émigré, was in hospital in Lincoln with frostbitten hands and feet. He would be lucky if he only lost fingers and toes. Two ops into his first tour his war was over.

"A couple of feet further aft and the tail plane would probably have fallen off," Adam observed, bending down to get a better view of the damage to the underside of the fuselage. Group Captain Alexander nodded solemnly. Rufus had caught up with them and Adam fought him off, playfully.

"The new Senior WAAF will be reporting for duty on Monday," announced the Old Man. "Did I tell you I got a letter from Squadron Officer Laing, by the way?"

"Er, no, sir."

"A very pleasant letter. About how much she had enjoyed her time here. Wishing us luck, and so on. I never did get to the bottom of why she put in for a transfer."

Adam coughed. "No, sir?"

"No. Anyway, it seems she's been posted to Lindholme."

A mile away a Merlin barked into life. "Looks

like Tilliard's putting his sprogs through their paces, what!" Alexander exclaimed, cheerfully.

Adam heard a second Merlin firing up. Today was one of those days when the Group Captain's indefatigable good humour was almost more than a man could bear. He slowed his steps, lit up a cigarette. This morning - post op - his hands were steady, rock steady.

They walked on.

It was a grey, dull morning. The clouds were gathering over the high wold and although rain was not forecast until nightfall, the air was damp and cold. The weather was supposed to be clearer in the north where Tilliard was taking his sprogs. The first Lancaster was rolling around the perimeter road, its sprog pilot sweating over the throttles. Tilliard would be standing over his shoulder, talking, advising, cajoling.

"Stay off the brakes... Low revs on the inners, steer with the outer Merlins... That's it, gun number four for a couple of seconds... See how she straightens up... Keep off the brakes except in an emergency..."

Two other Lancasters lurched forward, jolted onto the road.

"You must give my regards to Ellie," said the Group Captain.

"Yes, sir." Adam was mindful that the Old Man was a regular visitor to the Rectory, a family friend of the Naismith-Parry's and long before his own arrival on the scene the Rector and his wife had virtually adopted Eleanor and her children. No matter how hard he tried to separate the world of the Squadron and the world outside the gates of the airfield the two grew inexorably ever more entwined.

Alexander jammed his pipe between his teeth as he gazed across the aerodrome. The fluky, southerly wind snatched at his coat tails. G-George was lining up for take-off. The pitch of her Merlins rose as her pilot eased the throttles up to zero boost against the brakes, and fell again as he throttled back. In a moment the Lancaster was rolling, Merlins racing.

"Have you had any further thoughts on what we were discussing yesterday, sir?" Adam asked, changing the subject. Group planned to increase the number of Lancasters operating from Ansham Wolds by expanding 647 Squadron's establishment from two, to three ten-aircraft flights. This could be achieved at relatively short notice by creating a third, C Flight, from cadres withdrawn from A and B Flights, by transferring all unassigned - so-called odds and sods - aircrew to the new Flight, and by filling the gaps in the ranks with sprog crews drafted directly from the Group reserve. Inevitably, this would spread the Squadron's old lags perilously thinly. Adam had broached the subject and the available remedies with the Station Master the previous afternoon, just before the off.

"We've discussed this before," Alexander said, wearily. "I'm sorry, Adam. I won't sanction poaching. That's final."

"Fair enough, sir."

"Everybody's in the same boat," the Old Man continued, attempting to soften the pill. "Poaching other squadron's old lags isn't on. I hope we understand each other?"

"Yes, sir." Poaching was *verboten*. Adam had of

course, realised that Alexander would want to play the game with the straightest of straight bats. Which was precisely why he had gone out of his way to make the 'poaching case' yesterday, laying the ground work for an alternative option which was, in any event, his own preferred way forward. "In that case," he went on, smoothly. "We need to consider who is ready for advancement from within the Squadron. If and when we have to start filling the gaps, sir?"

"Quite."

Too late Group Captain Alexander realised the younger man had backed him into a corner. The poaching issue was a red herring, a ruse to box him in, and to soften him up for the sucker punch. Like a fool he had walked right into it.

Chapter 9

Friday 19th November, 1943
St. Paul's Church Hall, Ansham Wolds, Lincolnshire

Eleanor looked up to find Adam framed in the doorway. She had been tidying away the chairs, getting ready to lock up the school and to take Johnny and Emmy home. It was four o'clock, the other children were long gone and the school week was over.

"Hello, again," he said.

Eleanor smiled, smoothed down her frock.

"Why, Wing-Commander, I thought you were avoiding me?"

"Goodness gracious, no!" He protested, mildly, leaning against the door frame, cap pushed back at a rakish angle. "I waved as we went by, yesterday. Well, actually, the chaps did most of the waving. They don't like me taking my hands off the controls. Not when we're down on the deck like that."

Eleanor laughed.

"The children were awfully impressed."

Adam sauntered into the Church Hall.

"And what about their teacher?"

"Well, I suppose I was a little bit impressed," she confessed, ruefully. "Just a little bit. Ever such a little bit."

"Only a little bit? In that case I'll fly lower next time."

"Don't you dare!"

He bent his face to hers and they kissed. Without inhibition she threw her arms around his neck and fell into his embrace.

"Don't you dare," she repeated, breathlessly in his ear. The man hugged her, briefly lifted her off her feet. "Johnny and Emmy will be wondering where I am," she remembered with a start. "They'll want their tea."

Adam had paid his respects to the Rector and his wife, said hello to the children on his way up to the Church Hall. The youngsters were playing in the low, walled garden behind the house.

'Eleanor will be locking up about now,' the Reverend Naismith-Parry had told him. 'I say, one of your chaps did a most spectacular fly past yesterday morning. Most exhilarating! Wing-tips literally brushing the tree tops all the way down the valley!'

Adam had tried to hide his embarrassment.

'Surely not, sir. That would have been most irregular.' Politely fending off an invitation to stay for tea he had gone in search of Eleanor. He craved a moment of normality, sanity.

Earlier that afternoon he had driven to Lincoln and visited Y-Yorker's injured gunner at the County Hospital.

Sergeant Janek Borowski had come to Britain in 1938, aged fourteen. His family had fled Sudeten Czechoslovakia hours ahead of the Wehrmacht, lost everything. Janek and his elder brother Juri, had both joined the RAF. Juri was two years older, a navigator on a 4 Group Halifax. Adam had spoken to Sergeant Percival, Y-Yorker's pilot before he set off for Lincoln and the story had come out in dribs and drabs. Borowski's family were Jews. In the boy's great grandfather's time

Czarist pogroms had driven the family out of White Russia, to Poland, thence southward. His father, now an interpreter attached to the War Office, had fought in the Austro-Hungarian Army in Italy in the Great War.

Borowski's bed was curtained off at the end of a long, high-ceilinged ward. Adam's feet had echoed loudly on the polished floor. The doctor said the boy was sedated, in pain, but fully aware of what had happened to him. There was concern about the risk of secondary infection. He could lose a hand or a foot, or worse. It was too early to tell.

'In these cases septicaemia is often inevitable, possibly leading to the onset of gangrene, you see.'

His gunner's face was red, blotchy, scalded by the icy blast of the cold at twenty thousand feet over Saxony. The boy's eyes widened as his CO slipped through the white curtains, stood over him.

'Hello, there.'

Borowski tried to sit up. Adam held up a hand, smiled. He wanted to cry, wanted to scream at the injustice of it. Instead, he put on his best bedside manner and radiated stern sympathy like a scoutmaster comforting a boy with a blistered heel. The gunner's hands were swathed in thick crêpe bandages.

'Will I fly again, sir?' The boy had asked him.

'Perhaps. That'll be up to the medics. When you're back on your feet. But that won't be for a while. I'm afraid you won't be going anywhere for a while.' Adam recollected speaking to the boy the day he joined the Squadron, over a month ago. The boy's dark, intense eyes and his heavily accented English had marked him apart from the other members of his crew. 'Is there anything I can do?'

The young Czech thought about it.

'Please, sir. Will you write to my father?' The boy lifted his ruined hands an agonized inch off the bed. 'I no write for while, sir. Only not tell him his son hero. Just, his son and his English friends, they bomb Big City. We bomb Big City good. Ya, sir?'

Adam had leaned forward, patted the boy's shoulder.

'You and your friends,' he grinned. 'You bombed it good.'

'Ya, we bomb it good, didn't we, sir?'

Adam nodded. "Yes, you did."

The boy smiled, soon afterwards he had slipped into a fitful, drugged sleep. While he drifted in and out of consciousness Adam had drawn up a chair, sat with him half-an-hour, and left when the boy seemed to have sunk into a deeper, more peaceful slumber.

Driving north along Ermine Street the roads had been clogged with convoys of lorries and tankers. Bomber Command was re-stocking its arsenals. Bombs and bullets and fuel, spare parts and new crews were on the move to feed the great, rapacious maw of the Main Force. Last night the Lancaster Force alone had burned 2,500 tons of 100-octane petrol and dropped 1,500 tons of bombs. The Lancaster Force was getting bigger, stronger and hungrier day by day; consequently, the convoys and the traffic jams were growing also, grinding down the narrow Lincolnshire lanes, rumbling past the peaceful fields, hauling their cargoes of death...

Adam helped Eleanor stack the last few chairs, checked that the windows were shut tight and helped her on with her coat. Her hands brushed against him, a stray strand of her hair touched his cheek. He waited patiently while she pad-locked the door. He took her hand in his as they crossed the yard to the gate.

"Do you have to rush off?" She asked as they walked down the steps to the Rectory.

He shrugged, apologetically.

"I'm expected back."

They stopped at the gate.

"Come and see me tomorrow," Eleanor prompted, hopefully. "If you can. We could go for a walk. Up to Ansham Hall, perhaps. The children love it up there."

"If I can get away," he promised. "I'd like that."

"Good."

"I won't come in."

"Tomorrow, then," Eleanor said, brightly. Adam gazed into her brown eyes. The wind blew her hair awry, across her face. Instinctively, tenderly he brushed it away, kissed her mouth softly, lingeringly.

"Tomorrow."

Chapter 10

Friday 19th November, 1943
RAF Ansham Wolds, Lincolnshire

Lancaster Force at maximum effort to the Big City, a handful of heavies missing in the morning and Ansham Wolds' solitary casualty, a frostbitten gunner. Yet it still felt like defeat. The gods of war were mocking the Main Force.

Adam smoked a cigarette in the quietness of his room.

He kept thinking about Janek Borowski. About the anger burning in the darkness of Janek Borowski's young eyes. The anger that put him to shame as he read again the letter he had written to the gunner's father.

Dear Mr Borowski,

By the time you receive this letter you will already have received a separate telegram informing you that your son, Janek, has been injured in the course of bombing operations against Germany.

Earlier today I visited Janek in hospital in Lincoln. Please let me assure you that he is in good hands and is receiving the best possible care. As a result of damage sustained by Janek's aircraft from a direct hit over Berlin, he has suffered severe frostbite to his hands and feet, and to a lesser extent, also to his face. It is with much regret that I must tell you I have been advised by the medical staff looking after Janek that it is likely he will lose some or all of his fingers and toes. I am further led to believe that while Janek's life is not in danger, he will probably be in hospital for some time. I have also been told that it is unlikely that Janek will ever recover sufficiently be deemed fit to return to active service.

Last night Janek flew as the rear gunner in a Lancaster flown by Sgt. Pilot Percival. This aircraft was in the forefront of the attack on Berlin. Janek is a very brave young man and given the nature of his ordeal over Germany last night, very fortunate to be alive.

Although Janek was not wounded by the anti-aircraft shell which disabled his aircraft, despite the best efforts of other members of his crew he was trapped in his turret and it was not possible to extricate him until after his aircraft had landed back at base. In all he was trapped for some five-and-a-half hours.

Throughout his ordeal Janek conducted himself with great courage and dignity. This is all the more to his credit because he knew that had his aircraft crashed he would have been unable to bale out. When I saw Janek, he asked me not to tell you that he was a hero. Rather, he asked me to report to you that your "son and his English friends bombed the Big City." And that "they bombed it good!" Sir, let me confirm to you that Janek and his friends did indeed, bomb Berlin "good"!

Janek joined the Squadron in early October. He and his crew had already made their mark. Although last night's operation was only his second, in both the operations in which he participated, against Dusseldorf at the beginning of this month, and in last night's attack on Berlin, his crew pressed home their attack with conspicuous bravery and determination.

May I take this opportunity of passing on to you my hope that Janek makes a swift recovery from his injuries.

Please do not hesitate to let me know if there is any way I can help you.

Yours sincerely,
Adam Chantrey
Wing-Commander, Commanding, No. 647 Squadron

The boy's pride touched a chord, mocked Adam's old lag's cynicism. To the exiled Czech gunner bombing Berlin was a special thing, a great and honourable endeavour in which he had been happy and proud, privileged to play his part. Somewhere along the high roads to Germany Adam had lost his pride and his wonder, come to regard the blasting and firing of the faraway cities as a way of life, routine. Normal. A job to be done in cold blood, without a fanfare and without question. He envied Janek Borowski his innocence. Most of all he envied him his absolute belief in the justness of the cause.

There was a knock at his door. Group Captain Alexander's new WAAF driver entered, smiling, bearing a steaming mug.

"The Adjutant said you'd appreciate this, sir," the woman stammered, nervily.

"Thank you," he said, indicating that the woman should put the cocoa on the corner of his desk. Whenever he had his light on late at night a WAAF would appear, a hot drink in hand. "Group Captain Alexander got back safe and sound, then?" He inquired. The Station Commander had attended a bash in the Mess at Bawtry Hall that evening.

"Yes, sir."

Adam grinned. He avoided formal Mess Dinners like the plague, cried off with whatever excuse came to mind. This evening's affair had been scheduled some while ago and nothing short of a maximum effort show would have caused a stand down. Hours on end dressed up like a clown and forbidden to talk shop was not Adam's idea of having a good time, hardly fun. Had he been a real career man his abhorrence of such bean feasts might have been a fatal handicap. Tonight, he had volunteered Barney to chaperon the Old Man. His second-in-command had been as pleased as punch with his assignment and jumped at the opportunity.

Barney was welcome to it.

He sighed, stifled a yawn.

Chapter 11

Saturday 20th November, 1943
RAF Ansham Wolds, Lincolnshire

Group Captain Alexander was in good form that morning. Excellent form despite the wind angrily buffeting the windows and the squally rain noisily lashing the corrugated iron roof.

"Blasted weather," he complained, gruffly. The Squadron's Lancasters were parked at dispersals and the Main Force stood down for the day. "We've got the Hun on the ropes but we can't finish him off because of the damned weather!" This said, he paused to sip his tea. His eyes were bright, glistening with fighting spirit after his evening at Bawtry Hall.

"Yes, sir," Adam said, dutifully. In his humble opinion 'the Hun' was nowhere near being 'on the ropes'. In boxing parlance, the enemy was bloodied but distinctly unbowed, soaking up body blows without ever looking – not for a single moment - as if he was in danger of going to go down for the count.

"You missed a damned fine bash last night! Pity you were under the weather. Feeling better this morning, I hope?"

"Yes. Thank you, sir. Much."

The Group Captain reached for his pipe.

"Yes," he went on. "Everybody was in high spirits. The other night's show was a pretty fair opening shot, what? Four hundred Lancs bombing in the Berlin area, only nine aircraft missing.

Damned good start, I say!"

Judiciously, Adam kept his mouth firmly shut. Even if Thursday's raid had been a 'good start' - which it was not and the Station Master knew it - they would have to repeat it night after night if the German capital was to be brought to its knees.

"Oh, by the way," Group Captain Alexander announced. "As per the grapevine effective the beginning of December, 647 Squadron will convert to three flights."

Adam blanched. The timing was something of a bombshell, he had hoped for another month's grace.

"As soon as that, sir?"

"Afraid so. We're to raise a C Flight from our existing personnel and resources. Group don't think aircrew availability will be a constraint, the OTUs are turning them out in their droves. But aircraft may be a problem. What do you think?"

Adam hesitated.

"I hadn't anticipated that Group would be in such a hurry, sir."

"Well, they are and we've got to get on with it! I've got my ideas on how we ought to proceed," Alexander declared. "No doubt you have your own. I'd like to hear them, now."

Adam had fished out his cigarette case. The match flared.

"The way I see it, sir," he prefaced, exhaling thoughtfully. "Is that we already have a C Flight, albeit in a putative form. The Conversion Flight. Under Peter Tilliard's command the flight has been up and running for the best part of six weeks."

Group Captain Alexander was momentarily

speechless. His thoughts had turned around promoting one of Barney Knight's senior pilots, either the South African, Barlow, or in extremis, Mick Ferris, the Ulsterman.

"Peter Tilliard?"

"Yes, sir."

"I agree the Conversion Flight approach may be worth pursuing. But Tilliard? Is that wise? What about the other candidates? I can think of at least two chaps with more experience and seniority?"

Adam had seen this coming, prepared his ground well in advance.

"Mick Ferris or Henry Barlow," Barney Knight's oldest old lags, "for example, sir?"

Alexander nodded, eyebrows narrowing.

"Sooner or later," Adam continued, "Barney's going to get his own squadron, sir. When that happens either Mick or Henry will step into his shoes. May I speak frankly?"

The Station Commander frowned, recognising belatedly that he had been as comprehensively outflanked as he had suspected the previous day.

"Of course."

"The last thing I want is for C Flight to be created as a pale shadow of B Flight. What we need is a new broom. If C Flight was already up and running I'd have no objections to promoting either Barlow or Ferris to command it. However, it does not exist, and building up a flight from scratch is a completely different kettle of fish from inheriting a going concern."

The Group Captain sat back. "Granted. But why Tilliard? Mac has one or two capable old hands if you're worried about contaminating the new flight with B Flight's bad habits?"

"I always envisaged the Conversion Flight as Peter's stepping stone to replacing either Barney or Mac when the time came, sir," Adam explained, making no pretence of apology.

"Did you by God!"

"Yes, sir."

Group Captain Alexander clasped his hands in his lap.

"I take it that's your recommendation, then?"

"Yes, sir." Adam waited for the explosion.

It never came. The older man put on his stern face, grunted, got to his feet and turned to gaze out of the window into the falling rain.

"Have you mentioned this to Barney or Mac?"

"No, sir."

"Good. I need to think about it."

It was then that Adam knew he had prevailed.

Chapter 12

Saturday 20th November, 1943
The Gatekeeper's Lodge, Ansham Wolds, Lincolnshire

Adam braked the Bentley to a skidding halt in the mud outside the cottage. Ahead of him the overgrown gravel road twisted into the trees and climbed the side of the valley behind the Gatekeeper's Lodge. Although the rain had blown over for the moment, Group had warned that the leading edge of the next Atlantic weather front was due before evening.

"Stay," he growled at Rufus. "You stay there, old boy." The Alsatian slumped down in the foot well, and eyed him accusingly.

Clambering out of the car, Adam gathered up his sheepskin flying jacket from the passenger's seat, slung it over his shoulder and made his way between the puddles to the door. Wispy, grey smoke issued from the chimney, water dripped off the thatched roof. He knocked on the door, once, twice.

It was Jonathan who opened the door to let him in out of the wet.

"Hello, young man."

"Come on through!" Eleanor called from the kitchen. He did as he was bade, hanging his sheepskins on the hook in the hall. "I didn't expect you so soon," the woman exclaimed, happily, planting a pecking kiss on his lips. She was wearing her housecoat, her hands and forearms were covered in flour. There was flour on her cheeks, in her hair. "I've been making bread," she said, looking down at herself. "And some scones, for tea. I must look a proper sight!"

"You look beautiful."

Eleanor blushed.

"I'm sorry I had to rush off yesterday," he went on, "I wouldn't have been very good company." Without intending to he explained about his visit to Lincoln, Janek Borowski and the letter he had written to the gunner's father. The story spilled from his lips as Eleanor moved about the kitchen.

"Oh, the poor boy," she said, when he finished his tale.

"He's lucky to be alive."

The woman set about washing the flour off her hands and arms. The man watched as she dried herself, took off her housecoat, smoothed down her blue dress. The warmth of the range seeped slowly into his bones.

"I met Squadron Leader McDonald in the village this morning," Eleanor announced. "He was on his way to Thurlby Junction to collect his wife. She's staying at the Sherwood Arms for a few days."

"Really?" Mac had gone into his shell since his rear gunner had been killed. Adam had left him to his own devices. To do anything else would have been an unwarranted intrusion, an insult. Hopefully, his wife's arrival would cheer him up.

"I bumped into Ben and Round Again, too. Outside the Sherwood Arms!"

"Ah, that I can believe."

Eleanor filled the kettle, positioned it over the hot plate. "How on earth did that sweet boy come to be called 'Round Again'?"

Adam toyed with a white lie, convinced himself that he might safely risk the truth. So, very matter of factly, he explained.

"It was over Cologne, back in July. Things were a bit dicey. The Pathfinders were unloading TIs, target indicators, all over the shop. As they do, sometimes. Angus was a bit wet behind the ears in those days. He got a tad confused. He asked if we could go *around again*."

"Oh. And did you?"

Adam sat down at the table. "Go around again?" He shook his head. "Goodness, no! Jolly dangerous, that sort of thing. We leave that sort of thing to the Yanks. They're the ones who think they're heroes!"

Eleanor put her hands on her hips.

"You're not pulling my leg, are you?"

"I wouldn't dare."

She came over, sat lightly on his lap. Her lips brushed his brow.

"So, when you flew down the valley the other day? Was that dangerous?"

"No," he replied, honestly.

Flying a Lancaster over water at sixty feet at night was fairly dangerous; stooging round Danzig Bay searching for a German aircraft carrier in the fog was rather more than ordinarily dangerous; flying with sprogs was bloody dangerous, positively ill-considered. Testing out the altimeter on the deck over Lincolnshire on a clear, sunny day was a breeze.

"Good," she said, quietly.

He circled her waist, drew her near before he

noticed Emmy standing in the door, viewing them curiously in the fearless way that only young children can. Adam smiled, winked at the girl and suddenly, Emmy was very self-conscious.

"Come in and say hello, dear," Eleanor suggested and the girl approached, let her mother pick her up. Emmy fingered the medal ribbons and the faded pilot's wings on Adam's left breast.

"Uncle Adam," Emmy asked, directly, gazing up into his face. "Are you and mummy going to be married?"

Adam did not know what to say or do.

Eleanor rescued him.

"Only if it's meant to be, darling," she said, patiently. This seemed to satisfy Emmy. Fortuitously, the kettle boiled, and Eleanor eased the child to the ground.

"Oh, I brought Rufus, today," Adam remembered. "I hope you don't mind. I thought the exercise would do him good."

"Bring him in!" Eleanor insisted, not daring to meet his eye.

"If you're sure." Outside, he attached the dog's lead and took a close hold on it as he brought his big black wolf of a German Shepherd into the Lodge. To his surprise Rufus was a deal more worried by Johnny and Emmy than they were by him. Little by little Adam relaxed his grip on the dog's leash.

"Oh, he's an old softy," Eleanor said, tickling Rufus's ears.

The Alsatian wagged his tail, and continually looked to his master for reassurance.

"How old is he?" Asked the woman, kneeling

beside the dog.

"About four, I think. I sort of inherited him."

"Inherited him?"

Adam parried the question. "I'm his third or fourth master." A responsible dog owner on ops always ensured that he included his man's best friend in his will. Otherwise, some zealous basket working for the Committee of Adjustment was liable to have your man's best friend gifted to strangers or worse, put down, the moment anything happened to you. Accordingly, within days of taking command at Ansham Wolds Adam had bequeathed Rufus to Tom Villiers. Just in case. "He's been with me about eighteen months, now."

"Oh, I see."

Eleanor's children were petting, stroking and prodding Rufus unmercifully. He put up with it stoically. He licked Emmy's face, she laughed ecstatically, threw her arms around the dog's neck.

"Does he fetch?" Johnny asked.

Only if you stand him a half of stout, Adam said to himself.

"If he's in the mood."

"All dogs fetch things?" Eleanor put in. "Don't they?"

"He's a bit of a Mess dog, I'm afraid."

Eleanor had to prise the children off the Alsatian to dress them for the wet, muddy outdoors. Then, leaving the boy and the girl in Adam's charge she disappeared briefly, returning a few minutes later attired in old slacks and a thick woolly jumper.

"Not very alluring, I'm afraid," she apologised.

"You'd be surprised," he retorted, grinning.

Eleanor lowered her eyes.

Adam collected his flying boots from the Bentley, donned them and his sheepskin flying jacket before they set off. The trees were bare, their leaves lying in wind-blown, damp heaps on the ground. Rufus loped off into the near distance with Johnny and Emmy running after him.

Eleanor reached out and squeezed Adam's hand.

"Ansham Hall was stripped bare when Harry's people left. The Bank boarded it up and ran the estate from an office in Kingston Magna and then one night there was a fire. It's just a shell, now. A ruin, really. Very gothic. I should imagine it's quite eerie at night."

Adam had flown over the ruins of Ansham Hall many times. It was an invaluable landmark. One that was impressed on every sprog crew the first time they flew one of his Lancasters. Underfoot their feet crunched on gravel, and foliage encroached on the disused driveway. Around the corner a tree had fallen, blocking the road. They picked their way up the gentle slope, avoiding the puddles, carefully stepping over broken branches.

"The old estate is huge on the map?"

"It was about nine or ten square miles," she informed him. "A lot of the land purchased by the Air Ministry for the aerodrome was originally Grafton land."

The shell of Ansham Hall stood proud against the sky as they emerged from the trees. The mock battlements reared high above the long abandoned sun terrace. Broad steps led up to the great doorway. One great oaken door swung wide open, hanging precariously on its rusted hinges, betraying the rubble-strewn courtyard within.

"It doesn't look so big from a couple of thousand feet," Adam observed, idly. At ground level it looked like it had been visited by the Main Force.

They stopped on what had once been the croquet lawn below the Hall. Now saplings had taken root, shrubs had sprouted, weeds had overwhelmed and eradicated the immaculate, lovingly cultivated turf.

"If things had worked out differently you might have been the mistress of all this," the man remarked, glancing sidelong.

"If," she sighed. "I wouldn't have enjoyed it, though."

"No? Being the lady of the manor?"

Eleanor laughed.

"No, I wouldn't have enjoyed being the lady of the manor. Not one little bit!"

"Why ever not?"

"It's not me, that's why not!" She protested. "I'm not the Squire's daughter-in-law, I'm Ellie Merry from Oxford. And I always will be!" They trudged up the muddy slope towards the brooding ruins. The children went ahead of them, foraging in the bushes, chasing each other's shadows, calling out in play. "Besides, I don't believe in all this nonsense about the Squire, or the Lady of the Manor. All that stuff belongs to another age. Like the dinosaurs."

"My word. That sounds positively socialist," Adam chuckled.

Eleanor fell silent.

"Have I said something wrong?"

Eleanor met his gaze.

"No," she replied, shaking her head. "Harry was a Communist." This said she made a second confession. "A proper one. A card-carrying member of the Party."

Adam raised an eyebrow.

"The Communist Party?"

"Yes. Are you shocked?"

He shook his head. Not a lot shocked Adam these days.

"Harry was a dreamer," Eleanor went on. There was a bitter sweet wistfulness in her as she spoke. "He wanted to go to Spain. To join the International Brigade. Luckily, I managed to get pregnant with Johnny. That made him see sense. I don't think anything else would have."

"That's the sort of thing that tends to concentrate a chap's mind, I should image," Adam offered.

Sadness filled her eyes.

"Harry never really forgave me, of course. It was his one chance to take part in a great crusade. It would have given his whole life meaning. And I spoiled everything."

"I don't understand?"

Eleanor bit her lip, avoided his stare. The breeze plucked at her raven, black hair, strands blew across her face. She brushed them away, distractedly.

"I didn't want him to go to Spain. So I stopped him going. I stole his dreams and afterwards he was never the same. I got my way; I kept him safe at home. The only trouble was that afterwards, I lost him little by little, every day until he finally went overseas. He got his wish in the end. He died fighting Nazis, after all."

Adam shrugged, pursed his lips.

"Spain was a lost cause. What we're doing here is different."

"You think so?"

"Yes, I do. I've never been much of a one for politics. Politics is what you do when you're not trying to blow the other fellow's head off." Adam gazed past Eleanor into the heart of the crumbling facade of Ansham Hall. "I take it the Prof never knew about Harry? And his, er, affiliations?"

"No," she confirmed. "Can you imagine the scandal if father had ever discovered his daughter was married to a fellow traveller?"

Faraway, the sound of Merlins drifted across the wold. A single aircraft, heading north. Some idiot braving the elements. In places the cloud base was down to ground level.

"So, what other secrets have you been keeping from me?" Adam asked, a twinkle in his eye, fun in his voice.

"None, darling. None whatsoever."

She led him up to the steps of the big house. Treading carefully through the fallen masonry they clambered onto the rubble-strewn terrace. Back down the slope the trees parted in the east, opening onto a broad, spectacular vista of the misty valley below.

"More to the point, what secrets have you been keeping from me?" Eleanor prompted, teasing him.

"Nothing in particular," he assured her, rather too quickly.

"Children!" Eleanor called. "Leave Rufus alone!

Come away from the house! You know it's not safe!"

Adam peered hard into the swirling mists. A bank of low cloud was slowly rolling in from the east, enveloping the woods and the ruins of Ansham House in its clammy embrace. There would be storms tonight, no ops tomorrow. One more day on earth for the men who would not return from Berlin the next time.

Eleanor shivered in the gloom.

"Children. Come over here where it's safe..."

Chapter 13

Monday 22nd November, 1943
RAF Ansham Wolds, Lincolnshire

Adam was awakened from a dreamless sleep by a shaft of dawn filtering into his quarters through the narrowest of gaps in the black out curtains. Exactly as the meteorologists predicted the storms had passed by in the night and the weather had broken. Tonight, the Main Force would almost certainly return to the Big City.

Adam marched into his office a little after eight that morning, attacked his in tray. Shortly the call to readiness would clatter up on the Operations Room teleprinter, so he focussed on his paperwork with a methodical urgency. He would be informed immediately if there was any news. In the meantime he wanted to keep busy and besides, whatever happened over Germany the red tape never went away.

At nine o'clock Mac stuck his head around the door.

"Thought you like to know, sir. We're on for tonight."

Adam looked up, poker-faced.

"All section heads to report to the Ops Room in fifteen minutes, please," he directed. "Has the Station Master been warned?"

"Yes, sir."

"Very good." With which Adam went back to his in tray. Appearances were everything. The chaps took their lead from him. His job was to keep things on the straight and narrow, calm and not to get over-excited.

At the door Mac hesitated a moment, then, with the glimmer of a wry smile and a shake of the head he departed. He understood the game the Wingco was playing; on ops days Bert Fulshawe had rampaged around the station like a rogue elephant with a huge flea in his ear.

Alone again Adam put down his pen and unable to contain his restlessness, jumped up, and began to pace. Fifteen minutes! In fifteen minutes he would walk into the Ops Room as cool as a cucumber. In fifteen minutes he had to have collected his thoughts, his wits and his fortitude. In fifteen minutes his people expected him to lead them into battle and it was his duty to be word perfect, foot perfect.

In command.

The preliminary operations order did not specify a target. It was too early for that. No matter, it had BERLIN written all over it.

"The Big City?" Barney asked, reading the teleprinter tear off over his CO's shoulder as the Operations Room filled with bodies. The word had gone out that all available aircraft were to be flight tested by 13:00 hours.

"Probably," Adam conceded. "If not Berlin, then maybe Leipzig, again. Definitely somewhere in that part of the world." He glanced up at the Readiness Board. Currently, 647 Squadron was showing twenty-two aircraft with crews available for operations. It was a new record. Other 1 Group squadrons would also be boasting unusually high aircraft availability, courtesy of the low-level of operational activity in recent weeks.

<u>URGENT IMMEDIATE - ALL SQUADRONS</u>

No. 1 Group Operations Order 43/11/6a

Information. - All Squadrons should come to readiness to participate in a major attack.

Executive. - GOODWOOD.

Operating Restrictions. - Lancasters I and III. Under no circumstances are all-up take off weights to exceed 66,000-lb.

Fuel. - 1,950 gallons

Bomb Loads. - Total available bomb lift will not exceed 10,050 lb., to be made up as follows:

Fifty percent of aircraft are to carry 1 - 4,000-lb. H.C., 2 - 1,000-lb. M.C. or G.P., maximum economic incendiary loads.

Twenty-five percent of aircraft are to carry 1 - 4,000-lb. H.C., 4 - 500-lb. M.C. or G.P., maximum economic incendiary loads.

Twenty-five percent of aircraft are

to carry 1 - 4,000-lb. H.C., maximum economic incendiary loads.

Bomb Fusing. - All 4,000-lb. H.E. bombs are to be fused tail inst. Of the 1,000-lb. and 500-lb. bombs carried, 75 per cent are to be fused TD .025, and 25 per cent are to be fused long delay with No. 37 pistol. Long delay fuses will be varied up to the maximum delays available.

Orders concerning the target, route, method of attack and codename to be used in respect of this operation will follow. All normal preparations should be commenced immediately.

ACKNOWLEDGE RECEIPT BY TELEPRINTER.

GOODWOOD signified a maximum effort. All available aircraft were to participate in the operation. The revised authorised take-off weights accommodated an increase in each aircraft's bomb lift from the previous Berlin attack. On that night Adam's Lancasters had carried maximum fuel, 2,154 gallons and a reduced bomb load of 8,500 pounds. The extra fuel had been required because of the circuitous route home over central and southern Germany. Tonight, he surmised, the Chief was contemplating a straight in, straight out route; shortening the trip by at least two hundred miles and an hour's flying time. By reducing fuel loads and arbitrarily increasing take-off weights, the bomb lift of each of his Lancasters had been increased by nearly three-quarters of a ton.

The composition of the bomb loads was standard but the fusing instructions caught his eye. All cookies and 75 per cent of the other high explosive bombs were to be fused to explode on impact, or within .025 of a second of impact, which was pretty much the same thing. This was the standard procedure. However, 25 per cent of the 1,000 and 500-pound bombs were to be fitted with delayed-action fuses, an unusually high proportion. Normally, only about 5 to 10 percent of bombs would be fused for delayed detonation, with settings varying from a few minutes to several days after impact.

Adam rubbed his chin.

"If it is Berlin, again, we'll leave as many sprogs at home as possible." Even as he said it he suspected it would be the last time he would be in a position to shield his sprogs.

"Absolutely, sir."

"Excuse me, sir," squeaked a nervous WAAF, standing timidly at Adam's elbow. The girl looked like she ought to be wielding a hockey stick, not working shifts in a bunker in Lincolnshire plotting the downfall of the Third Reich.

"Yes, what is it?" Despite the business in hand Adam spoke softly, gently to the girl. On ops days people watched his every move, gesture, and read things into the inflexion of his voice and the way he held himself. This morning he found half a smile from somewhere and the WAAF lowered her eyes.

"It's the new Padre, sir." The young woman had never spoken to the Squadron Commander before.

It was her first day on the Ops Room Staff and to most of the WAAFs on the station the famous Wingco was a remote, distant figure more like a movie star than a mortal man. She swallowed, tried to remember what else she had been going to say. She hesitated, on the verge of panic. However, when the Wingco simply smiled a wry, patient smile, she relaxed, and suddenly remembered exactly what she needed to say. "The new Padre, sir. He's waiting upstairs, sir. Outside, sir. He says you asked him to report to you this morning, sir? But the guard won't let him in. On account of the fact he hasn't got a pass, sir."

"Thank you," Adam murmured, dismissing the WAAF, who fled instantly. Turning to his Flight Commanders he allowed himself a brief: "Blast it!" And wanly confessed: "I knew I'd forgotten something. Barney, be a good chap and order the sentry to let the Padre into the Ops Room."

His second-in-command hurried off, laughing.

Damn! The new Padre had reported to Ansham Wolds the previous Thursday morning. He had sent the newcomer a welcoming note yesterday suggesting perhaps that they might have a chat in his office at nine-thirty that morning. Then the Ops Order had materialised.

"Ah, Padre," he smiled, greeting the newcomer, bypassing the older man's salute and sticking out a welcoming hand. "I do apologise. I gather they wouldn't let you in. Bad show. My fault entirely. I should have had a word with the Adjutant. Made sure you had the run of the station. I'm terribly sorry."

Flight-Lieutenant the Reverend Richard Poore

was a cadaverous, balding man of indeterminate middle years. Melancholic by nature his first few days at Ansham Wolds had shaken him to the core. Since his arrival he had been in limbo. Nobody had paid him the least attention, nor given him a second glance. Everybody was busy. A bookish, introspective man not gifted with an outgoing nature he had wandered the station like a lost soul, pushed from pillar to post, if not actually shunned, then unnoticed.

"Thank you, sir," he said, at once disarmed and hugely relieved by the obvious sincerity of the welcome and the unequivocal fulsomeness of the youthful CO's apology in front of an audience that was clearly comprised of the majority of the Squadron's senior officers. Contrary to what he had been told at Group Headquarters, Wing-Commander Chantrey seemed, on the scanty evidence of this belated first acquaintance, to be anything but the aloof, cold-eyed tyro he had been warned to expect.

The Padre had been in the RAF three months and had only himself to blame; his parishioners in Cheltenham having been astonished by his sudden announcement that he had been called to serve in 'another way'. His health was not robust, he could honourably have stayed in his Parish for the duration, enjoyed the security of his living, and hidden away from the tragedy of the age. But that would never have done. Only his wife, bless her, had understood that he could not idly sit by.

The Air Force had inducted him, sent him on a brief course in Grantham, thence to Bawtry Hall. Nobody had known what to do with him at Group

Headquarters where he had discovered, quite by chance, that Ansham Wolds had due to the illness of its incumbent Padre, a vacancy. Approaching the Wing-Commander (Personnel), he had pleaded, implored, and begged to be posted to 647 Squadron until such time as the incumbent was restored to full health.

The Wing-Commander (P) had tried to talk him out of it.

Thinking about it afterwards that had been a most curious interview. The mere mention of Ansham Wolds seemed to agitate the man, simply speaking the name of 647 Squadron's famous CO had had him reaching for a cigarette.

'Be a good fellow, why not wait for a vacancy to arise at a more, er, *normal* station?'

He had refused to be swayed, and now here he was.

In the lion's den.

"I went to your office, sir," the Padre explained, falteringly. "They said you'd be in the, er, Ops Room. But when I got here they wouldn't let me in."

Adam sized up the new Padre. The Reverend Poore's predecessor was in a tuberculosis sanatorium, unlikely to return to active service. The new Padre had about him the look of an undertaker which was not good.

"No, bit of a flap on today," he grinned. "We're on for tonight."

"Oh, I see. Would it be better if we had our, er, chat, another day, sir?"

Adam shook his head.

"No. No time like the present, Padre."

"If you're sure. I don't want to get in the way."

"Barney," Adam called, half-turning. "Can you organise some flying kit for the Padre?"

"I'll get right onto it, sir," acknowledged his second-in-command, grinning broadly.

The Reverend Poore shifted uneasily.

"Come with me," Adam declared, "let me show you around your Parish, Padre."

Leaving his second-in-command to oversee the preparations for the coming night's entertainment, Adam led the older man up the steps and out into the cold brightness of the morning. He paused, took a couple of long, deep breaths.

"Have you ever been up in an aeroplane, by the way?"

"Er, no. I can't say I have..."

"Don't worry. We'll soon put that right." Adam sauntered towards his Bentley, opened the passenger door. He completely missed the momentary look of abject horror on the Reverend Poore's ashen face. "Hop in, Padre."

The car rolled forward, rapidly picking up speed. Soon they were careering across the airfield, the wind roaring in their faces, the engine racing, wheels squealing, spinning, skidding on the frosty ground.

"I'm sorry if I've neglected you," Adam re-iterated, raising his voice above the racket. "I like to get off on the right foot with people and it's my fault entirely if we've not got off to a good start."

The Reverend Poore clung on for dear life as the Bentley scorched over the tarmac. He had no idea where he was being driven to, or why, and was swiftly becoming a little disorientated. He said nothing. Listening was his great strength; possibly the reason why he was such a dismal sermonizer. He listened, now.

"I'm not a very religious chap. Not as such," Adam went on. "But if there is a God, I believe that *He's* on our side. I believe also that it's important that our chaps believe that *He's* on our side." Near the southern boundary of the airfield the Bentley lurched to a halt beneath the towering nose of a Lancaster. The two men looked out through the mud-spattered windscreen and beheld the broad, sunlit panorama of Ansham Wolds. "Do you know the Reverend Naismith-Parry?"

"I'm afraid I don't."

"He's the Rector of St. Paul's. I'll point it out when we fly over the village later on," Adam said, staring into the distance. "The Reverend Naismith-Parry's son was killed on Stirlings. He holds certain views on what we are about here. He has every right to hold those views, of course. Every right. Nevertheless, it would be inappropriate for him to express those views within the confines of the station."

"Ah," sighed the Padre as the penny dropped. "And you are concerned that I might share some, or all of his views, sir?"

Adam nodded, he did not need to elaborate.

"The Reverend Naismith-Parry's views relate, I take it, to the morality or otherwise, of the bombing of Germany?"

"Yes."

"I see," said the Padre. He sensed this was a make or break moment. Damage done now would be impossible to repair. Any misunderstanding, any dissembling was unlikely to be forgiven or forgotten. "And you wish to know where I stand on this?"

Again, Adam nodded.

"I think all war is an abomination, Wing-Commander. All war is a tragedy. But I'm not here to fight. I'm here to minister to the men and women of this station."

"Mind if we stretch our legs, Padre?" The younger man got out of the car, offered the Reverend Poore his cigarette case.

"Thank you, no. I don't, sir."

Adam lit up, strolled towards the menacing black bomber sitting squarely on its hard stand.

"We'll be flight testing the old girl in a couple of hours. Twenty minutes across country. Nothing exciting. We'll head out over the coast, test the guns. You come along for the ride, Padre. It'll give you a chance to see the chaps at work."

The Reverend Poore was a lifelong martyr to vertigo. The thought of climbing a ladder reduced him to a quivering wreck. Now, standing beneath the port wing of the Lancaster he realised for the first time that these aircraft were very, very *big* and he suddenly wondered: how on earth they could possibly fly?

"Is that not against regulations, sir?"

Adam heard the quiet alarm in the man, shrugged.

"Absolutely."

The older man plucked up every last ounce of his failing courage.

"In that case I should be honoured to er, come for a ride with you and the, er, chaps, sir."

"Capital. That's the spirit." Adam wandered under the nose of the bomber, his eye searching for the slightest blemish, anything out of place. He stopped directly under the starboard inner Merlin, reached up and touched the lower limb of the great, three-bladed propeller. "We're probably on again for Berlin tonight, Padre."

"Yes, sir."

"Another Goodwood show."

The cleric looked askance at this.

"Maximum effort, Padre," he was informed. "All available aircraft. Possibly all Groups. Over seven hundred heavies. Everything but the kitchen sink, in layman's terms."

The Reverend Poore was silent.

"We got off lightly on Thursday night and the chaps know it," Adam confided. "When we went to the Big City in August and September we lost upwards of seven percent of the kites we despatched. A hundred and twenty heavies in three shows. That was then. This is now. This time we're going to keep going back until there's no more rubble to turn. Whatever the cost. Don't let the chaps pull the wool over your eyes. They know the score. A chop rate of seven percent wipes out a Squadron every fourteen or fifteen ops so the chaps don't need to be mathematicians to work out the odds." He paused, pursed his lips. "You'll find we don't talk about these things among ourselves, Padre. Not much point, really."

The Padre shivered.

"No. I suppose not."

"Anyway," Adam sighed, breaking the circle of his darkling thoughts. "The thing is, I won't have anybody standing in judgement of *my* crews, or what they're about. I just won't have it."

The Reverend Poore took this in his stride. A lesser man might have taken profound exception.

"I was in the trenches in the First War, Wing-Commander," he said, sadly. "Afterwards, I turned to the cloth to try and make some kind of sense out of the madness. Turning to God seemed the most natural thing even though there had been times, many times when I had cursed Him, and believed with all my heart that He had forsaken me. I'd volunteered at the beginning. I was on the Somme."

Adam said nothing.

The Padre's voice shook as he spoke.

"We went over the top at dawn. Over five hundred of us. Half the battalion was dead in minutes. By dusk less than fifty were still alive, most of us were wounded. When it was dark those who could crawled back through the wire. I was sent to England to convalesce, then back into the line. At the third Battle of Ypres, Passchendaele, I was gassed. Not too badly, I was one of the lucky ones. The wind veered soon after the gas reached our trenches. I was blinded but only for a week or two. After that they decided all I was good for was the Staff. My Division was in the line when Ludendorff launched his great offensive in April 1918. Our forward battalions were over-run immediately and I was sent forward to see what was going on. The Germans had broken through. It was chaotic, hopeless. I came upon the positions of a battalion of my old Regiment, the West Middlesex Yeomanry. They were dug in across the road to

Amiens. The Colonel recognised me, and called me over. We chatted a little while, about our Harrow days, I recall. And cricket, oddly enough. Then the German barrage started to fall in the woods around us. 'Well,' the Colonel said, 'you better be on your way, young Poore. Please be so good as to inform the Corps Commander that in the absence of orders to the contrary, the battalion fought to the last man.' I shook his hand and I ran away."

Adam took out his last cigarette, lit up, inhaled.

"They were all killed?"

"Yes. Most of them, yes." The Reverend Poore was shocked that he was daring to speak of these things. He had buried them deep, locked them away; lived in terror of naming his demons lest they rose anew to devour him. Yet there was a strength in the younger man that bolstered his courage and steeled him to face those demons. "So, you see, Wing-Commander, I am here not so much to judge, but to atone."

Adam viewed him thoughtfully, smiled a wan smile.

"Welcome to Ansham Wolds, Padre," he said. "Take it from me, this is as good a place as any to atone."

Chapter 14

Monday 22nd November, 1943
RAF Ansham Wolds, Lincolnshire

The Reverend Poore would have fallen but for the strong, willing arms of the erks waiting outside the fuselage door. His blind panic ebbed, his stomach churned.

"Are you all right, sir?" Asked a worried fitter.

The Reverend Poore shook his head, fended off the supporting hands and stumbled to the tail, where he leaned on the wing. The other members of O-Orange's crew were decamping from the Lancaster in the leisurely, cheerful way they had gone about their business throughout the half-hour test flight. The Padre's world was spinning slowly. He was going to be sick. Very sick. He was about to make an ass of himself and there was nothing he could do about it. He retched uncontrollably, vomited agonizingly on his shoes, trousers and the ground by the tail wheel.

"Steady on, Padre," said a friendly voice. The large, gentle hands of the navigation leader guided him to the steps by the fuselage door, sat him down. "I thought you were looking a tad peaky."

The Reverend Poore attempted to speak. No words came, his throat was dry, constricted. The dreadful dizziness passed and becoming aware of the mess he had made of himself, felt ashamed and humiliated. Ben Hardiman's steadying hand remained clamped protectively on his hunched shoulder.

"You must think I'm a fool?" He blurted.

"Not a bit of it, Padre," the big man assured him. The other members of the crew were gathering in the background.

"Feeling a bit fragile, Padre?" Adam inquired, jumping down to the tarmac, peering over his navigator's shoulder. "Touch of air sickness?"

The Reverend Poore's head was clearing.

"I shall be fine, really." To illustrate the point he rose unsteadily to his feet, swayed drunkenly, managed to stay more or less upright. "Just a spot of vertigo, that's all."

"Vertigo?"

"I've always been a bit of a martyr to it, you see. It's nothing. Nothing, sir. I'm fine, now."

"You suffer from vertigo and you still came flying with us?"

The Reverend frowned in confusion.

"The *next* time I shall take the precaution of breakfasting lightly, sir."

Adam's lips slowly cracked into a wolfish grin for he and the Padre were going to be, if not necessarily firm friends, then at least allies in *this* enterprise.

Berlin was confirmed as the target at noon. The designated aiming point was situated in the Mitte District, close to the sprawling landscape gardens of Berlin Zoo. Approaching the city from the west the Pathfinders would fly over Stendal, establish an *H2S* fix over Rathenow, and carry on into the heart of the target area, passing between the Spandau and Tegel Forests in the north and the Grunewald in the south. The route overflew the vast *Alkett* tank works, *Siemensstadt,* with its hive of war industries, and the mainly residential districts of Charlottenburg and Tiergarten.

The mood in the Briefing Hall was grim that afternoon when Adam set the tip of his billiard cue tapping gently at the big, ugly smudge on the huge map of northern Europe.

"Berlin, gentlemen," he began. "Metropolitan area eight hundred and eighty-three square miles. Pre-war population over four million, probably less now. A lot less. The other night we had all sorts of trouble finding a TI to bomb. Had it not been for your press on spirit the raid would have been a failure. So tonight, new tactics will be employed over the target. I believe that these new tactics will make a *big* difference."

Last Thursday's attack had of course, been a fiasco. That was ancient history. The important thing was that the Pathfinders were out to make amends. Hence the new tactics.

"Tonight," he went on, "the Pathfinder Force will be led by a small force of Special Blind Markers. These Specials are Lancs equipped with the latest version of *H2S*. Each Special will carry four red TIs, four yellow TIs and sixteen Sky Markers."

The new version of *H2S* operated at a wavelength of 3 centimetres and allegedly, provided much improved resolution over built up and wooded areas.

"The Blind Marker Force will be split into two separate groups. Group one will be the Openers. They will lay down the initial blind marking pattern. Group two will be the Backers-up. These aircraft will back up the initial marking effort throughout the raid, refreshing existing markers, if necessary on *H2S* indications alone. If at any stage in the attack the marking becomes scattered the Backer-up crews have been ordered to back up the red and yellow TIs dropped by the Special Blind Markers. All Pathfinder aircraft will drop both TIs and Sky Markers."

The crews listened in silence, heads nodding. Old lags looked at each other, exchanged knowing winks. What was being proposed made eminently good sense. Blind marking would continue throughout the attack and regardless of the weather conditions over the target the deployment of Sky Markers would guarantee that some markers would always be visible.

In theory.

"Tonight, there will be a further departure from the normal drill," Adam told his crews. "Each crew will be given its own individual bombing time. The most experienced crews will bomb early, the less experienced, later in the attack. The same principle will be applied to the Halifax Force, and the fifty or so Stirlings which will be operating tonight. Make sure you keep to the time you're allotted. The bombing window is only twenty-two minutes."

Previously, each Group and each type of aircraft had been allocated its own wave, separating Lancasters from Halifaxes and Stirlings. The abandonment of this practice was bad news for the Halifaxes, and extremely bad news for the Stirlings. Over Berlin the Lancaster Force was liable to be bombing through five-tenths Halifaxes and Stirlings.

Adam's sympathies went out to the Stirlings who would be flying a mile below the lowest

Halifaxes. But only in passing. He had worries enough of his own. While welcoming the long overdue revision in tactics the changes fell well short of what he, and many other old hands, believed was necessary. The maddening thing was that Bomber Command had successfully - and famously - toyed with the missing piece of the Pathfinder jigsaw over six months ago. The situation cried out for a Master of Ceremonies in unbroken communication with both the Pathfinders and the Main Force; a *Master Bomber* with the authority to command and control the *whole* attack over the target. Guy Gibson had done the job with 617 Squadron over the Ruhr dams in May; John Searby had done it during the Main Force attack on the Luftwaffe Experimental Establishment at Peenemunde in August. However flexible the Pathfinders' pre-ordained tactics, without a Master of Ceremonies there was always far too much scope for a monumental cock-up.

Adam put aside his reservations and dismissed the crews. Tonight's GOODWOOD was not going to go off half-cock. Not if he had anything to do with it.

Chapter 15

Monday 22nd November, 1943
RAF Ansham Wolds, Lincolnshire

Jack Gordon threw himself onto his cot to partake of his pre-op nap. This afternoon he was strangely restless and he turned to his friend.

"Writing to Suzy, again?" He asked, innocently.

"Yes," Peter Tilliard grunted, settling himself at the wobbly table.

"Oh." Jack was ambivalent about his pilot's attachment to Suzy Mills. All things considered it was probably better to remain unattached. "Don't you run out of things to say? Writing every day, I mean?"

Tilliard glanced at him. "No, not really."

"Oh. Must be the real thing, then," the Australian observed, dryly.

It provoked an irritated sigh from the other man.

"I should hope so!"

Jack smiled to himself: it was no good, his friend was bewitched. He reached for his cap, pulled it down over his face and shut his eyes. He had solemnly ruled out all possibility of lasting entanglements with a member, or members of the feminine sex. That was, nothing that went beyond a fling. There was nothing wrong with a good naughty once in a while. But nothing serious. Nothing with a future. After the war there would be plenty of time for doing the decent thing. If there was an 'after'. The way things were shaping up 'after' was beginning to look increasingly iffy now that maximum efforts to Berlin twice a week until the spring seemed to be the order of the day; bad news for a chap with most of his tour in front of him. Decidedly dicey. Men fought temptation in different ways. Jack Gordon's patented method was to periodically remind himself that statistically, he was a dead man. A dead man walking, maybe, but still dead...

"Anyway," Peter Tilliard reminded him, "I recollect that Nancy Bowman was all over you the other night. I didn't see you fighting her off."

Jack sighed. There was no denying it. The buxom eighteen year old younger daughter of the Landlord of the *Hare and Hounds* had a well-developed soft spot for him. Right between her ample breasts. He would have to be strong. It was a test; God's way of finding out what he was really made of. The first sign of weakness would be his downfall and he knew it. If Nancy once discovered a crack in his defences he would be finished.

"Ouch. Low blow, sport," he complained.

Tilliard shook his head, returned to his letter to Suzy.

Dearest Suzy,

Op number twelve upcoming. The Big City again. This will be a short letter because we're off early again today. Personally, I prefer an early 'off'. Hanging about gets on everybody's nerves.

I may soon be free of the Conversion Flight. The Wingco's asked me to see him tomorrow morning to 'have a quiet word' about 'things'. Several new crews have arrived in the last few days. It's getting a bit rich, all these sprogs floating around and nowhere near enough serviceable kites for them to fly.

Jack's a cynical fellow, you know. I was having a little moan about us having sprogs coming out of our ears, and he turned around and said I shouldn't worry about it because 'the Chief was working on it'. I suppose he was thinking about this new start we've made with the Big City. Jack's a fine fellow but sometimes I wish he'd keep his opinions to himself!

Jack seems to have taken a shine to Nancy Bowman (Bill Bowman's daughter). We went down to the Hare and Hounds last night and it was the first time I haven't had to carry Jack back blind drunk. It was something to behold - Jack on his best behaviour. Well, what passes for "best behaviour" with Jack. I don't think Jack quite knows what to make of things. Further reports as the plot develops!

This morning I got your letter of the 15th. I'm sorry to hear you've got another head cold. I hope it was just a twenty-four hour thing this time. I'm glad you've decided to tell your people about us (well, a little bit about us!). I think you're a lot closer to your people than I am to mine and I suspect they worry much more about you than mine do about me.

I woke up this morning thinking about the

last time I saw you. I felt as if you were with me and I longed to be waking up beside you. It may sound silly, but I often feel you are with me, watching over me. And thinking it makes everything else so much easier.

Tilliard put down his pen.

Tonight, S-Sugar was due over the target at 08:06, eight minutes into the attack. It was time to dress, pull on thermal underwear, a thick white sweater under his battledress, flying suit, don his boots and gloves and go to war.

Unlike Jack he eschewed the paraphernalia of an escape kit. Everybody was supposed to collect a basic escape kit from the flight room on the way to the buses but like many men he never bothered. Jack however, religiously lugged his own personal big 'evader' rucksack out to the aircraft. In it he carried civilian clothes, a pair of sturdy walking shoes, silk maps, emergency rations for a week, a small bottle of whisky, a service revolver, two dozen rounds of ammunition, a compass, a first-aid kit, an English-German phrase book, a needle and thread, a crow bar, scissors, and coins of several denominations in a variety of currencies. The rest of the crew suspected he had other items – presumably of a nefarious nature - stashed away in the darker recesses of the bag, but Jack got very tetchy whenever anybody attempted to inspect the rucksack.

"When we get shot down I'm going to walk to Switzerland," Jack would declare. "While you blighters are cooling your heels in some *Stalag Luft*, yours truly will be playing the field in Geneva!"

Tilliard did not see much point in putting together an escape kit. If they were hit he might be able to hold the aircraft straight and level long enough for the others to bale out, personally he accepted that he had a negligible chance of surviving. The moment he released the controls the bomber would plummet, dive, tumble, spin. He would be pinned in his seat or hurled around the inside of the Lancaster. Either way he would be trapped.

It was best not to think about it at all.

He folded the letter for Suzy, addressed the envelope, and placed it unsealed on the table. When he got back he would add another page or two in time for it to catch the mid-day collection from the Mess. He got up, shook Jack Gordon's shoulder.

"Wakey, wakey, old man."

The Australian pushed back his cap, sniffed the air.

Aircrew superstition dictated that the forms of the rite had to be meticulously obeyed.

"Show time," Tilliard said, smiling a very thin smile.

Chapter 16

Monday 22nd November, 1943
The Gatekeeper's Lodge, Ansham Wolds, Lincolnshire

Late that afternoon Kate McDonald came to the Gatekeeper's Lodge. Around lunchtime, hearing the Lancasters taking off and landing, Eleanor had sought her out at the Sherwood Arms and invited her to tea. Kate was a pale, waif-like girl, not yet twenty and pregnant. Eleanor had taken pity on her immediately. Mac's young wife was a long way from home and suspecting that her husband would be otherwise engaged that evening, she had taken it upon herself to befriend the girl.

The Lancasters were taking off as Kate walked down the lane past St Paul's Church. The light was failing fast, the heavens trembled and shook to the droning of Merlins on high. She had thought nothing of the Lancasters coming and going earlier in the day. Now with a horrible sinking feeling she realised the activity had been the prelude to a raid. Which was why, she belatedly surmised, Mrs Grafton had invited her to tea.

The sound and fury of the bombers climbing over Lincolnshire chilled her soul, recalling the terrible night three years ago when her family's terraced house, and most of the rest of the street had been demolished by a stick of German bombs. The target had been the Glasgow docks and the worst bombing had fallen on Govan where her father was working his shift. He had survived, but it was nearly a week before they dug her mother out of the ruins.

It was not long before Kate was telling Eleanor the whole story and its sequel: how she had met her husband, on whom she unashamedly doted. The women and the children sat around the table in the kitchen, Eleanor poured tea, and tried to persuade her guest to nibble at a scone.

"So, when's the baby due?" She inquired.

"The end of March."

"Emmy's birthday is in March. Mac must be delighted?"

Kate smiled at this, blushed.

"I think so. Even if he wasn't he wouldn't show it. That's the way he is."

"Your families?" Eleanor prompted, gently. "You said your families lived just a few streets apart but you never met Mac until you were bombed out?"

"Three streets away," Kate explained. "I knew Maggie, Mac's sister, who was killed the same night as my mother. Just to say 'hello' to. She was three or four years older than me. I'm a Catholic, you see. Mac's not. You don't know what that's like living down here. The men worked together in the shipyards and the factories, but there were different schools, different churches... Anyway, they said there were four bombs, they fell in a line, knocking down about twenty houses. The gas main in our street caught fire. It was awful. We didn't have a cellar or a shelter nearby and there weren't any public shelters near where we lived. We'd always thought we were safe because the docks were miles away."

"It must have been awful?"

"I was at the top of our street when the bombs came whistling down. I got blown across the road. When I picked myself up the street wasn't there anymore. There was just smoke and fires, dust. Dust in my eyes, in my nose, in my throat. Some people were running, some were standing still. There were bodies lying in the road, and there was rubble everywhere. On one side of the street there was a house with two old folks trapped, we tried to put out the fires but we couldn't. They were burned to death. The fire brigade never came and there was no water. The water main in the next street was burst. A direct hit. When it started to get light I looked for mother but the house had collapsed, sort of fallen in on itself. I knew she was under the wood and the bricks but there was nothing I could do."

Eleanor sipped her tea, let the girl talk.

"The Church took us in. Catholics and Protestants. All of a sudden nobody cared what you were. It came on to rain that day and the roof of the church was damaged. By the blast, you see, and it leaked. But there wasn't anywhere else to go. We were all a bit dazed. We'd lost everything. Nobody really knew what was going on, nobody was in charge. The council didn't do anything for us for three days, and then they said they wanted to evacuate us. They were still digging people out, so I wouldn't go. I couldn't, not until they found mother."

Eleanor tried to imagine what it must have been like for a slip of a girl whose world had been wiped off the face of the earth, her mother killed and her family put out on the street. It was beyond her imaginings. It was too frightful.

"But your father was all right?"

Kate smiled sadly.

"After the funeral he signed papers on a steamer. I haven't seen him since. He doesn't even know Mac and me are married."

"Tell me about Mac?" Eleanor murmured, trying not to sound too horrified.

"Mac's folks died before the war. His sister, Maggie, she'd just got married. Her husband, Billy, he worked in the yards, somewhere on Clydebank. Mac had just finished his basic training. He had a seven-day pass and he was coming up to stay with Maggie. He arrived the week after the raid. Practically everybody in Maggie's street was killed, so there was nobody who could even tell him she was dead. He went to the church to find out what had happened to Maggie. When he walked through the door I was the first person he saw."

Eleanor nodded. "Would you like some more tea, Kate?"

"Please, a little."

"A scone?"

"No, thanks. I'm sure they're lovely but I won't."

"Sorry, I interrupted you. Mac walked through the door?"

"He said who he was and asked me if I knew if Maggie and her husband were safe," Kate recollected, haltingly. "I had to tell him they were dead. I took him to see where they were buried. He took it bad, he cried in the cemetery. That's the only time I've ever seen him cry. Anyway, we got to talking. We hit it off straight away. He didn't have any money or anywhere to stay. All the people he knew were dead or evacuated so he stayed the rest of his leave at the church. He was marvellous. He went down to the council offices, got them to put a tarpaulin over the leaking roof, he got them to issue everybody new ration books, he wrote letters for people, he went with the wee ones and the old folk to see their relatives in hospital. He sorted out the funeral arrangements for mother, he made sure things were done decently and that she was buried properly. I don't know what I'd have done without Mac. I think it was love at first sight. Does that sound all wrong? I mean it was such a horrible time. But as soon as I set eyes on Mac I knew things would get better, you see. That was before I even knew his name. I didn't know how, but I just knew things would get better."

"So, how long have you been married?"

"A year tomorrow," Kate said proudly. "We ought to have got married sooner, but Mac kept putting it off. He thought I was too young, you see. I don't think that matters. If you love each other you love each other and that's all that matters, don't you think?"

"Absolutely," Eleanor agreed, rising from the table to clear away the children's places. Johnny and Emmy departed into the parlour, leaving the women alone in the kitchen.

"Oh, I'm sorry," Kate exclaimed, thinking she had upset her host. "Mrs Bowman told me that your husband was killed last year. And here I am blathering on about Mac! I am so sorry! What must you think of me?"

"There's no need to apologise, Kate," Eleanor

assured her in her most soothing, maternal voice. "Really." Lancasters were climbing over Lincolnshire. The air hummed with the throb of their engines. Involuntarily, she turned and lifted her eyes to the ceiling.

Kate McDonald followed her eyes.

"I never realised it was like this," she admitted. "So many bombers, so much noise. Mac hardly ever talks about it."

"No. None of them do."

"I used to think it was because Mac wanted to protect me," Kate said, not suspecting that she and Eleanor had fears in common. "But I think it's more than that. Don't you?"

"Yes, I do. That's not to say I begin to understand it, though."

Kate rose and helped clear away the rest of the cups and saucers.

"I hope there isn't another raid tomorrow night."

"That would be too much," Eleanor sympathised. "On your first anniversary, of all nights!"

"Do they often fly two nights running?"

"Sometimes," Eleanor was bound to admit.

Together the women put the children to bed. Afterwards, they retired to the chairs by the fire, chatted harmlessly to distract themselves, the younger woman doing most of the talking. Eleanor learned that Kate had spent twenty-one nights with her husband in the first year of their marriage. Mac's baby son, or daughter, had been conceived on their ninth or tenth night together.

"I think you're very brave coming all the way down to Lincolnshire to be with Mac," Eleanor remarked when the girl let slip that before she was bombed out of her childhood home she had never travelled more than five miles from Govan, and up until two days ago, she had never crossed the border into England. "I take it you still live in Glasgow?"

"No. I couldn't live there, not after what happened. Mac asked his Uncle Rob and Aunt Flora to take me in. They've got this farm in the Borders, near Hawick. It's not very grand, but I fell in love with it the first time I set eyes on it. Just like I did with Mac. I help out, I milk the cows, I look after the chickens, that sort of thing. Mac's Uncle Rob and Aunt Flora are quite old. They never had any children and they make a big fuss of me."

"It's lovely up there. But you must get lonely, sometimes?"

"I miss Mac but there's always things to do on the farm. I'm not a one for dancing and carrying on. Not now." This confession slipped out guiltily, reluctantly. "Except when I'm with Mac."

Chapter 17

Tuesday 23rd November, 1943
RAF Ansham Wolds, Lincolnshire

Acting-Squadron Leader Peter Tilliard stood in the crowd as 647 Squadron's Lancasters hurtled down the runway bound again for the Big City. A cheer went up, B-Beer was rolling; B-Beer with a sprog crew making its operational début. The wind was gusting hard from the north-west. B-Beer roared past. Already, N-Nan was lining up, her pilot gunning the outer Merlins. All around the perimeter road heavies rumbled and jolted into the queue.

'Ah, Peter,' the Wingco had smiled that morning, indicating that he should take a seat. His office had been cold and condensation had dripped down the end wall. 'It looks like we're on again for tonight. Same fuel and bomb loads as last night. Big City, I shouldn't wonder.'

Tilliard had baulked at the thought. Trips on successive nights to the Big City were without precedent. If they were on for Berlin again it marked a new, worrying departure.

'Surely not, sir?'

'We shall see.' The Wingco had lit a cigarette. 'You've done a first rate job with the Conversion Flight, Peter. A first rate job.'

'Thank you, sir.'

The CO had smiled, sternly.

'Don't go thanking me, yet. I've got another little job for you.'

'Really, sir?'

'Afraid so,' the Wingco had nodded. 'From the beginning of next month 647 Squadron will be operating as a three-flight formation. Our Conversion Flight will become a fully fledged C Flight. Some poor chap is going to have to build up another Conversion Flight from scratch, but that's not your problem. *Your* sprogs will need old lags in the background to show them the ropes. Between them the other flights are going to have to give up three or four experienced crews.'

Tilliard had gazed blankly at the CO. One moment the Wingco had been talking about the Conversion Flight, patting him on the back, the next moment the he was giving him the lowdown on the Squadron's forthcoming expansion. He felt as if he had missed something glaringly obvious.

'I shall talk to Barney and Mac about that in due course,' the other man promised, ignoring his subordinate's bewilderment. 'They won't like it but that can't be helped.'

'No, sir.'

'I'll leave it to you to set up a Flight Office.'

'Er, yes, sir.'

'I don't want you flying ops until C Flight's up and running, by the way,' declared the Wingco, in a tone which brooked no argument. 'Once you've got things up and running you can go and get yourself posted missing whenever you want. Until then you're grounded. No ifs, no buts.'

Tilliard was at a loss for words, not knowing what to say or how to react, or whether to trust the evidence of his ears.

'I'm sorry, sir,' he stammered like an idiot. 'I'm

not sure I understand?'

The Wingco had chuckled.

'It's a big job. One heck of a challenge, Peter,' he said, leaning forward in his chair. 'In many ways commanding a flight is a more demanding job, day in and day out, than commanding a squadron. However, I happen to think it'll be right up your street. That's why I've recommended that you be promoted acting-Squadron Leader and given command of C Flight. Officially, the new flight doesn't exist until the beginning of December, but I want you to get weaving first thing tomorrow morning. I shall be announcing your promotion and the creation of C Flight at the main crew briefing this afternoon.'

Tilliard had been dumbstruck. The Wingco had risen from behind his cluttered desk, walked around to take his hand in his own dry, firm grasp.

'Congratulations, Peter.'

It had still not really sunk in.

True to his word the CO had broken the news to the crews at the main briefing. Simultaneously an addendum to the day's standing orders was posted on all Squadron notice boards in confirmation. C Flight was to be formed around the existing Conversion Flight, supplemented by cadres to be drawn from A and B Flights. And: 'the new flight will be commanded by Acting-Squadron Leader Tilliard.'

'Bloody Hell!' Jack Gordon had whistled, turning pale.

Barney Knight had approached scowling mischievously, hesitated a moment, then stuck out his right hand.

'Congratulations, Tilly,' he had grunted. 'Good luck, old man. All for one, one for all. And all that guff!'

As Tilliard watched the Squadron's Lancasters roar off into the gloom the enormity of his unexpected elevation weighed leadenly on his shoulders.

R-Robert, the Wingco's kite, halted at the threshold. The deep, pulsing beat of her Merlins quickened as the throttles advanced to zero boost against the brakes. The Wingco throttled back, waiting for the signal to roll. Nearby, the Adjutant stood with the new Padre. The Wingco's Alsatian, Rufus lay at the Adjutant's feet, oblivious to the raging of the Merlins and the cheers of the crowd.

There was a party atmosphere out on the field.

God was on 647 Squadron's side and Bomber Command's star was in the ascendant. Truly, God was Great. Truly, the Main Force was His instrument. The Lancaster Force was climbing, climbing high into the night over Lincolnshire and setting its course for High Germany, His will to do. Tonight, anything and everything seemed possible.

R-Robert was rolling.

The crowd waved as one, hats and scarves raised aloft. The emotion of the moment caught in Tilliard's throat, tears welled in his eyes. The Lancaster Force was flying to Germany to confront its fate, to fulfil its terrible destiny. R-Robert picked up speed and her tail lifted off the runway.

Last night the Main Force had sown untold carnage in the streets of the Big City. Ten-tenths cloud on the route out, cloud tops up to sixteen thousand feet over Berlin had denied the crews any sight of land and grounded the night fighters. However, in the absence of the fighters the Pathfinders had flown into the worst of the flak and gleefully painted the aiming point with literally hundreds of Sky Markers. The Main Force had followed up with a concentrated bombing effort, the like of which had astonished many old lags. As the attack progressed the clouds below had begun to glow like mile upon mile of bloody cotton wool. Flying away from Berlin the eastern horizon had been coloured a sickly, deadly crimson by vast conflagrations burning out of control across the city. Tonight, the Chief was sending the Main Force back to stoke the fires of Berlin.

Tilliard shivered. Somebody was walking on his grave. It was at once Bomber Command's finest hour and the dawn of its darkest day. It was as if the unleashing of the whirlwind signalled a descent into some nightmare lower level of Hades...

"May I join you?"

Tilliard half-turned and discovered the new Padre at his shoulder.

The Wingco and the rest of his crew had – with one voice - given the Reverend Poore their unqualified and very public seal of approval. Tilliard strongly suspected that as a result the Padre had found himself walking on water these last few days, bewildered by his good fortune and a little daunted by the infinite possibilities newly revealed. The story about how the 'puking Padre' had concealed his lifelong vertigo from the CO and lived to tell the tale of his personal fearless 'corkscrew run' had become an instant Ansham Wolds legend.

"Be my guest, Padre."

"Quite a crowd, Squadron Leader." Observed the older man. "But I should imagine you'd rather be in the air than on the ground?"

"I should say."

The older man nodded.

"There will be other nights."

Tilliard watched P-Popsie rush down the runway. The rising crosswind caught the bomber as it unstuck. The heavy drifted left, port wing dipping perilously close to the grass. Her Merlins strained, her pilot struggled to correct the swing, and regained control. P-Popsie clawed away from the ground.

"Crosswind, Padre," he commented when he judged it safe to breathe again. "Makes life interesting, what! The wind wouldn't be so bad if it was steady. When it's gusting unpredictably like this it's a bit of a lottery."

The Reverend Poore was beginning to get used to the idea he was in the company of madmen. P-Popsie was the third aircraft that had almost come to grief. *Interesting.* It was more than interesting, it was more like Russian Roulette than a lottery. This sort of routine dicing with death defied reason. Courage in the face of the enemy, in defence of one's kith and kin, in defence of one's country and one's way of life, in defence of one's faith and in one's God was one thing, but this matter of fact, everyday intimate acquaintance – casually rubbing shoulders - with death was something else. Up here on the Wolds in the heart of England, in the midst of the county of flowers life was cheap.

"Will they stop the take offs if it gets any

worse?" He asked, shouting above the roar of Merlins.

Tilliard thought about it. Conditions had been borderline when the Squadron's Lancasters began to take off. The wind was rising, beating hard in their faces. The controller held the next Lancaster, Q-Queenie at the threshold, anxiously eyeing the windsock above his truck. The object of the exercise was to get the Squadron's heavies off, come what may. The controller had the authority to suspend take offs for a few minutes, only the Station Commander could call a halt to take offs. In these situations Wing-Commander Chantrey's first law of ops applied: if the weather is anywhere near flyable, "we fly". And that was that! As the CO had been heard to remark, more than once: 'Who wants to live forever, anyway?'

"No, we won't stop take offs," he decided. "Not unless there's a crash. Probably not then either unless the runway is blocked."

"Oh."

Tilliard realised that what he had just said probably sounded unspeakably callous to the Padre's untutored ear. Q-Queenie's Merlin's picked up. The Lancaster lurched forward and charged headlong into the gathering murk like an enraged bull.

"If we waited for perfect weather," he explained, "we'd never go flying at all at this time of year, Padre."

"No, I suppose not."

G-George was already in position. Even as Q-Queenie lifted into the air, crabbing sideways against the wind, G-George was rolling, engines surging deafeningly, racing the wind. Tilliard thrust his hands into his greatcoat pockets. The crews knew the score. 647 Squadron pressed on regardless. End of story. Nobody was overly keen about going straight back to Berlin. Nobody in his right mind liked taking off in an over-loaded kite in a crosswind but life was like that sometimes. The thing was to get on with the job; to get into the air and to do the business over the target. Hopefully, to get home in one piece. And survive. Survive until the next time. Life on the Squadrons was not as it was elsewhere and there was no point pretending otherwise.

The Wingco was right.

Who wanted to live forever, anyway?

Chapter 18

Tuesday 23rd November, 1943
Lancaster R-Robert, 25 miles NW of Minden

Despite the rafts of low broken cloud over their fields a large number of night fighters made contact with the Lancaster Force as it passed south of Oldenburg. Flying at the head of the bomber stream, hard on the heels of the openers, R-Robert droned on.

Last night 26 of the 750 heavies despatched to the Big City had failed to return. Another 6 aircraft had crashed in England or ditched in the North Sea. As usual, the lower flying Stirlings and the Halifaxes had suffered disproportionately higher losses in comparison with the Lancasters. All of Adam's crews had returned. Tonight might be very different: tonight might be a bloodbath. Tonight the Chief was courting disaster, daring the fates to do their worst.

Adam weaved the Lancaster from beam to beam, fought off the cloying embrace of his exhaustion. The cold was biting into his hands and feet, the roar of the Merlins surrounded him in a cocoon of noise and vibration. He had swallowed a brace of caffeine pills before the off but what he really needed was sleep, several night's uninterrupted sleep. Group Captain Alexander had politely requested he sit out this op and nine times out of ten he would have acceded to the Old Man's request. However, when the battle order clattered up on the Ops Room teleprinter at noon, he had put his foot down and asserted his right to participate in the show.

He had been so appalled by what the Chief was asking of *his* crews that there was no other honourable course of action open to him.

Not only was the Chief mounting a second major raid on Berlin within twenty-four hours, but in his 'wisdom' he had ordered the Lancaster Force to retrace last night's route to the Big City. For good measure both the timing of the attack, and the route home was also to be duplicated. Command believed - or rather, it had convinced itself - that the defenders would interpret the identical route and timing of the attack as some kind of elaborate ruse to conceal the fact that contrary to all the evidence, Berlin was not the real target. It was imbecilic. Half-baked, criminal. Even if the Germans thought the Main Force was going elsewhere, they would cover their bets, and mass fighters before the gates of Berlin. If Leipzig got flattened it was bad news, the local *Gauleiter* might kick up a fuss. If somebody gave the Lancaster Force a clear run to Berlin somebody's head would be on a pike outside the Brandenburg Gate the next morning.

The operations order was an open invitation to the crews to dump their cookies in the North Sea, and many crews had done just that.

Fifty miles out from Skegness the flashes of cookies erupting in the sea pointed the way to Germany. While it was normal to for the odd bomb load to be jettisoned by aircraft returning early due to mechanical problems, tonight huge explosions ripped up mile upon mile of empty sea. It was an ill-omen that unambiguously signified that many crews had decided they were being asked to do too much. It was not cowardice, simply pragmatism. The crews were not 'balking at the jump', as Adam had heard several desk-bound fools call it. The crews were not dumping their whole bomb loads in the sea and turning for home. They were simply lightening their aircraft to give themselves a better chance of carting their smaller HE bombs and their incendiaries to the Big City, and living to fight another day. Just because a tour on Lancasters had become a death sentence for most aircrew, why die sooner rather than later?

"Bloody hell! Is that the target up ahead, Skipper?" Ted Hallowes asked over the intercom, touching his pilot's shoulder and pointing towards the horizon. The ground was cloaked in cloud but in the distance the darkness of the sky was tinged with crimson.

The horizon literally glowed red.

"Pilot to crew," Adam called, laconically, pulling himself together. He shut his anger away in a dark place. When he had told the crew that they were flying again that night the chaps had looked him in the eye, nodded, and gone to collect their kit. Unwritten rules, ties that bind closer than blood, so many old lag loyalties that were unfathomable to outsiders. Tonight was going to be a bloody business. "You might like to know Berlin is still burning, chaps."

North of Brandenburg the flak groped for prey four miles high. R-Robert rocked and jolted through the barrage. Passing over Potsdam searchlights stabbed through jagged, miles-deep fissures in the clouds, dazzlingly, blindingly, terrifyingly. Momentarily, the bomber was coned, trapped in the hot, merciless beams of white light, before flying into the blackness beyond.

"Fighter flares, twelve o'clock high!" Ben shouted. He was standing at the back of the cockpit, an extra pair of eyes.

"Pilot to Navigator. I see them!"

The first flares sank into the flak. More fell in a long line across the burning city. Scores of Sky Markers were drifting down into clouds that boiled like a witch's cauldron. A few hundred yards to starboard a Lancaster flew into a wall of flak and ceased to exist. It exploded, disintegrated in mid-air. In the distance tracer arched through the flak, another heavy ignited and fell, drawing a plume of livid red flame into the clouds. The fighters were stepping to the Devil's tune, dancing in and out of the flak.

R-Robert bombed at 20:07. Her 4,000-pound cookie, three 1,000-pound general purpose bombs and nine hundred 4-pound stick incendiaries tumbled down into a blazing wasteland which until twenty-four hours ago had been the bustling residential district of Charlottenburg.

The clouds had denied R-Robert's bomb-aimer any glimpse of an aiming point in the streets of the Big City; Round Again had trusted to the accuracy of the Sky Markers. Far below vast fires raged out of control. Although the Germans sometimes lit giant decoy fires to draw the bombing effort away from the real target the conflagrations beneath the clouds could not possibly be decoys. Already in his young life Round Again had seen too many cities burning.

"Bombs gone!" He cried out. The cookie dropped first. A split second later the 1,000-pounders slipped away. Incendiaries spilled into the slipstream, falling end over end, scattering far and wide.

Cookies struck ground: great, supersonic shock waves rippled out across the clouds.

The Lancaster Force had begun to 'turn the rubble' of Berlin.

Chapter 19

Tuesday 23rd November, 1943
The Gatekeeper's Lodge, Ansham Wolds, Lincolnshire

Eleanor answered the knock at the door. The children had been in bed the best part of an hour and it had long been dark. She was not expecting a caller and had heard no vehicle in the lane.

She discovered Kate McDonald standing in the porch, shivering. She had been crying and broke down again as Eleanor opened the door.

"Kate, whatever is it?" She asked, instinctively reaching out to the girl. The younger woman sobbed as Eleanor guided her inside into the warmth of the parlour.

"It's Mac!" She blurted.

An icy hand clutched Eleanor's heart.

"What is it? Has something happened to Mac?" She prompted in a voice that was not her own. Kate McDonald sobbed and Eleanor hugged her. The possibilities were uniformly bleak. "Tell me what's happened?"

"Mac's had to go to Bawtry with Wing-Commander Chantrey."

For a moment Eleanor did not know whether to laugh or cry. Resisting the urge to shake some sense into the girl, she reminded herself how Kate doted on Mac. How little she had seen of him in the days she had been in the village. Yesterday had been Kate's first wedding anniversary and while she had worried herself ragged, Mac had probably been over Germany. Discovering that Mac had been called away on duty again tonight was too much.

"You mean Mac's all right?"

"Yes," Kate sniffed, shuffling back out of the older woman's arms. "You think I'm being silly, don't you?"

"No, of course not!" Inadvertently, Eleanor's voice carried a note of vexation.

"You do think I'm being silly. I'll go..."

Eleanor took a firm grip of the girl's hand.

"Kate, I don't think you're being silly. I really, really don't think that you're being silly. Believe *me* I understand exactly how you must be feeling."

The younger woman wiped away her tears with the back of a pale hand, her gaze full of mistrust.

"How could you?" She objected, sulkily.

Eleanor sighed. "I know how you feel about Mac because I feel the same way about Wing-Commander Chantrey." She had meant to say it with a certain steadiness, an absence of shrillness. Instead, she had said it plaintively, her words straight from the heart.

Kate's young eyes opened wide with honest astonishment.

"So," Eleanor went on, "I know what you've been going through every time you hear an aeroplane in the distance. And I also know how unfair all this must seem to you."

The younger woman had been startled out of her introspection.

"But you're older than..." Her words trailed away. "I'm sorry, I didn't mean it to sound as if..."

Eleanor smiled, wryly.

"Oh, yes, Kate. I'm much, much older, my dear.

Isn't it wicked?"

Kate could not help herself, she giggled.

"So," Eleanor went on. "You and I are both in exactly the same boat."

"I didn't know. I never guessed."

"Well, now you know." Eleanor sat her visitor in a chair by the fire, dropped two pieces of damp wood onto the embers, stirred the grate until the logs crackled and flames licked. She made a mental note to get somebody to cut more wood for the Naismith-Parry's. The coal ration was never sufficient at this time of year. Standing up, smoothing down her frock she viewed Kate maternally. "I know you can't stop worrying. It's only natural to worry. The trick is to try not to worry all the time."

Kate shrugged, remained silent.

"I try very hard not to worry about things I've no control over," Eleanor explained. "I'm lucky, really. I've got the school, Johnny and Emmy, the housekeeping for the Rector, the visiting I do in the Parish. I keep busy."

She made a mug of cocoa, laced it with a generous measure of the brandy that she kept for emergencies, and insisted the girl drink it. Kate wrinkled her nose.

"It'll do you good."

The girl submitted. At first, she sipped gingerly at the steaming brew, then, realising that she was not actually being poisoned, drank contentedly. The heat of the fire and the inner warmth bestowed by the alcohol slowly bolstered her morale. Presently, she managed to sustain a smile. When Eleanor went out into the kitchen for a few minutes she returned to find Kate asleep in the chair. Careful not to disturb her she fetched a blanket, spread it over her. Later she doused the parlour lights, kept vigil, reading a book by the flickering illumination of a single candle. She decided to let Kate sleep, the girl was exhausted from fretting, and in Mac's absence sleep was what she needed.

She heard the Bentley in the lane at around ten. There was a hesitant, polite knock at her door. Kate stirred but did not wake as Eleanor rose, and tip-toed past her towards the narrow hallway.

Mac stood in the porch.

"I'm terribly sorry to disturb you at this time of the night, Mrs Grafton," Mac apologised, painfully embarrassed. "But the Rector suggested I speak to you. I'm looking for my wife. She was staying at the Sherwood Arms, only she's not there. And I gather you've been so good as to befriend her..."

Eleanor put a finger to her lips.

"Kate's inside, Mac," she whispered. "She's sleeping."

The relief flooded into his troubled eyes.

"Thank God," he breathed.

"Don't worry," Eleanor assured him. "She's fine. Just a little tired, that's all. Come in. Come in." She shut the door softly behind the man. "I think Kate got a little upset when she thought she wasn't going to see you today."

Mac took off his cap.

"It couldn't be helped."

"I know. And so does Kate."

Mac nodded. He and the Wingco had been summoned to Group on a fool's errand to speak to two 'gentlemen of the press'. He had only been roped in because the moment the Squadron was stood down, Barney had departed to the fleshpots of Lincoln. The *gentlemen of the press* had turned out to be Americans, pleasant enough chaps but for reasons that were, quite frankly, beyond his ken, labouring under the ludicrous misapprehension that the American Eighth Air Force was winning the war single-handed. Not unnaturally, the CO had turned somewhat liverish.

'My crews have been to Berlin three times in the last week,' he had growled. 'Where was the *Fighting Eighth* when we were over the Big City?'

The new Wing-Commander (Operations), a jovial fellow, Freddie Tomlinson, had attempted to mediate. However, when he explained that the next time 647 Squadron was tasked to attack the Big City the 'gentleman of the press' would be flying with it, the Wingco had lost his rag in a big way. Mac had never seen the CO lose his temper. It was something to behold. Fortunately, it subsequently transpired that Freddie Tomlinson was an old chum of the Wingco's and he had taken it all in masterfully good spirit. He had soaked up the outburst; quietly suggested they adjourned to the Mess to continue the discussion. In private, over a stiff drink.

'Be a good fellow, try to see it as a feather in the Squadron's cap, as it were.' Freddie Tomlinson had sympathised, cheerfully. 'Oh, and the Deputy AOC wants to see you before you head back to Ansham Wolds, Adam.'

'Oh, joy!'

'Quite. He's off inspecting Ludford Magna at the moment. You'll have to hang around until he gets back, I'm afraid. As it happens we're having a bit of a bash in the Mess tonight. You'll join me, of course. I'd appreciate a bit of intelligent conversation with another old lag. Some of the desk wallahs around here haven't a clue. Not a bloody clue! Frightful shower! I imagine they must have driven poor old Pat Farlane up the wall!'

At this juncture the Wingco had tossed Mac the keys to the Bentley.

'No point both of us stooging around killing time, Mac. You get back down to Ansham. Off you go...'

Mac followed Eleanor into the parlour, looked down at his young wife sleeping peacefully in the big chair by the fire.

"Let her sleep a little more," Eleanor advised, softly. "Come into the kitchen and have a cup of tea."

"I didn't want Kate to come down here, to Lincolnshire," Mac said, lowly, closing the door at his back and stepping onto the cold stone flags of the kitchen floor. "There are things here it is best for her not to see."

"Ignorance is bliss?" Eleanor queried, smiling sympathetically. "Do sit down, you look worn out."

"Things have been a wee bit hectic, lately."

The woman topped up the kettle from the big jug she had filled from the well before dusk.

"Kate's a bright girl, Mac," she said softly. "Some things are easier to live with when you face up to them."

"Perhaps."

"I'm sorry. It's not my place..."

Mac grinned.

"No, it's all right. Really."

The door creaked ajar, inched open. Kate McDonald peered bleary-eyed into the kitchen. Roused by the sound of voices she was still half-asleep. Until, that was, she spied her husband, rising from the table.

"Mac!" She cried.

In an instant she had flung herself into his arms.

Chapter 20

Tuesday 23rd November, 1943
No. 1 Group Headquarters, Bawtry Hall, South Yorkshire

Air Commodore Crowe-Martin bustled into the ante-room of his office catching Adam unawares, dozing in a chair by the door. The younger man struggled to his feet, threw a shambolic salute.

"Come on in, Chantrey," rasped the Deputy Group Commander. "Sorry to keep you hanging around like this. You're a busy fellow, I know. Couldn't be helped, I'm afraid. Freddie's kept you entertained, I hope?"

"Yes, thank you, sir," Adam replied, stifling a yawn.

"What's this I hear about you making disparaging remarks about our colonial friends?"

"Ah. Well, sir. I, er, on reflection I may possibly have over-stepped the mark a tad, sir. Just a tad."

Crowe-Martin smiled a thin smile.

"No doubt you were provoked?"

"Somewhat, sir." To Adam's surprise the other man seemed genuinely amused.

"Never mind. Take a pew," the greying, dapper old fox said. "We won't stand on ceremony, this evening. The AOC has asked me to ascertain, confidentially, the views of the Group's senior Squadron Commanders on certain matters." With this Crowe-Martin fixed the younger man in his steely stare, his eyes unsmiling. "You've done a damned fine job at Ansham Wolds, by the way. It hasn't gone unnoticed." He did not dwell on the subject. "Is Knight ready for his own Squadron?"

"Yes, sir." Adam replied, unequivocally.

Crowe-Martin ruminated a moment. "What about McDonald?"

"Not yet, sir. He's a damned fine Flight Commander. But he needs more time."

The Deputy Group Commander paused, sucked his teeth.

"The AOC intends to advance Knight at the earliest opportunity. So, as soon as a suitable command falls vacant, Knight will be leaving Ansham Wolds. Given the sort of targets we shall be attacking in the coming weeks this probably means you will be losing him sooner rather than later, I should imagine. However, the AOC is concerned that nothing should undo the progress you've made with 647 Squadron over the last couple of months. Specifically, he is concerned that losing a man of Knight's calibre might adversely affect the Squadron's operational effectiveness."

"Nobody's indispensable, sir." Adam observed, poker-faced.

"My own view entirely," retorted the Deputy Group Commander. "Nevertheless, I have been authorised to let you know, informally of course, that should you wish to replace Knight with an experienced hand from outside the Squadron, the AOC would give the matter his full and most sympathetic consideration."

"That won't be necessary, sir."

"Good." Adam sensed the atmosphere undergo a subtle change of mood. The Deputy Group Commander crossed the first item off his agenda, and moved quickly onto the second. "I gather a number of crews jettisoned their cookies on the way out last night?" The words stuck in the older man's throat. Plainly, the implications of it were intensely distasteful to him.

"*My* crews pressed on, sir."

"I'm not pointing a finger, Chantrey!"

"No, sir."

The older man bit back his impatience.

"It won't do. It didn't happen on Monday night, why the hell did it happen last night?"

Adam ran his fingers through his tousled hair. His head ached from too many cigarettes and lack of sleep. He groaned inwardly.

"May I speak frankly, sir?"

"Yes."

"Well, sir," Adam organised his tired thoughts. If the Deputy AOC wanted to know why some of the crews had taken it upon themselves to even up the odds he would tell him. "The chaps watched the armour being ripped out of their kites. They got used to flying the new all-up weights. They even starting to get used to the idea that from here on in it is Berlin or bust. Given half-a-chance the chaps will get used to practically anything, eventually."

"Go on."

Adam braced himself.

"Last night the Chief asked the crews to do too much."

Chapter 21

Tuesday 23rd November, 1943
RAF Ansham Wolds, Lincolnshire

Suzy lay naked in his arms. The musky fragrance of her hair filled his senses as weak, watery sunlight crept through a gap in the blackout curtains. The sunshine fell coldly across the woman's bare, milky white shoulder. He nuzzled the nape of her neck, planted a kiss behind her ear. Suzy stirred, moaned softly and settled again. Her warm breath brushed his arm and he shrugged closer. Soon they would have to get up, dress, return to the world that they had known before. In a few hours they would be separated. Suzy to Shrewsbury, he back to ops.

'What time is it, darling?' She asked, sleepily.

'After eight.' She stretched against him, squirmed onto her side, looked at him, fondly. He gazed into her eyes, wanted to squeeze her to him, plunge into her anew only he was spent and she needed him to hold her tight. 'I love you,' he murmured.

She smiled, buried her face in his chest. The bed creaked. 'Oh, Peter,' she whispered. 'I wish we didn't have to go back...'

Peter Tilliard awoke with a start.

The dream instantly shattered into a thousand shards like a crystal glass hurled at a brick wall.

There was raucous banging, shouting and cursing in the corridor outside his room. The blissful peace of his dreams lost, he came back down to earth with a rude jolt. He switched on the light. The cold bit into him and as he struggled out of his cot, his breath frosted in his face. Jack Gordon's bed was made up, unslept in.

This was hardly surprising since it was Jack who was doing most of the bawling and swearing in the corridor. Sticking his head out of the room Tilliard saw that his navigator was being dragged backwards, feet bumping on the floor. Ben Hardiman held one arm, Barney Knight the other.

Jack had no trousers on.

"Ah, just the man!" Barney laughed, red-faced and barely coherent.

Tilliard glanced at his watch. It was four in the morning.

"The teetotal hero of *The Liberty* himself!"

"I take it you chaps had a good time in Lincoln, then?"

"Fucking marvellous," Ben Hardiman declared, nearly falling. He stuck out a hand, braced himself against the wall. "Fucking marvellous, old man! Ought to try it yourself!"

Jack was singing something incomprehensible. It might have been *Waltzing Matilda*, but the words were slurred and jumbled. A trickle of blood ran from his nose.

"Steady! Steady! Right five degrees! Steady!" Knight called. "Bombs gone!" With which he and the navigation leader simultaneously released their human cargo. Jack Gordon collapsed in a heap on the floor.

Tilliard frowned at his navigator's feet.

Jack's ankles were handcuffed together.

"Nasty little fracas," Knight explained, swaying

erratically. "I almost got away with a helmet. The Nav Leader here, he lifted the cuffs. That's style, what!"

"Absolutely. I don't suppose you've got the keys?"

Jack had fallen silent.

No, neither of them had the keys.

Tilliard accepted this phlegmatically. It had been too much to hope that they had the keys.

647 Squadron's second-in-command and Navigation Leader staggered off, leaning on each other for mutual support, leaving Tilliard alone with the prostrate body on the floor. Nobody else in the hut seemed to have been disturbed in the least by the rumpus.

"Sorry, old son," he muttered.

Taking a firm grip on his friend's collar, he dragged him into the room. Jack was out cold. Deciding against trying to get him into his cot, Tilliard turning him onto his left side, shoved a pillow under his head, threw a blanket over him where he lay and went back to bed. He would go in search of a hacksaw in the morning. Morning would be soon enough. It was not as if there was any danger of Jack sleepwalking. Not with his feet chained together.

Tilliard lay on his cot staring into the darkness, returned his thoughts to Suzy. She finished her ops course in less than a week and he planned to take her to Lincoln. Or perhaps, down to London. Yes, down to London and a proper hotel, not a damp, nasty hovel with cracks in the walls and a rickety old iron bedstead. This time he had had it all mapped out and then the Wingco had given him

C Flight. Now his half-made plans were in tatters. He had ceased to be a free man and Suzy had become a Squadron widow. He felt as if he was letting her down and their last conversation came back to him time and again.

'I could get pregnant,' Suzy had said, her face hidden in the gloom behind the hut. 'For all I know I could be pregnant, now...'

He had wrapped her in his arms until it was time to bid their farewells. In any other circumstances he would marry Suzy tomorrow but he had C Flight to build and a war to fight. Marriage was out of the question.

Or so he told himself, over and over again.

He missed Suzy desperately.

Chapter 22

Thursday 25th November, 1943
RAF Ansham Wolds, Lincolnshire

Faraway the rumble of engines in the night drifted down to earth but tonight the Merlins of the Lancaster Force were silent. Tonight it was the turn of the Halifaxes of 4 and 6 (RCAF) Groups to follow the Pathfinders to Germany. Adam lay on his cot and listened to the torrent of heavies streaming across the coast, climbing, climbing high above the churning North Sea.

That morning Ansham Wolds had been warned for the Big City. Preparations had been well advanced when the take off time was postponed. Then, after the crews had been briefed, eaten their pre-operation meal, dressed and been driven out to their aircraft the op had been scratched. The cancellation order had rattled up on the Ops Room teleprinter as the first Merlins coughed into life. A high-flying weather reconnaissance Mosquito had reported low cloud obscuring the target and convective cloud along the planned route. The combination of poor visibility over Berlin and the likelihood of severe icing conditions on the way out had persuaded the Chief to stay his hand, to err for once on the side of caution.

Meanwhile, the Halifax Force - over 200 strong - was off to turn the rubble of Frankfurt-am-Main, and until the Halifaxes returned Ansham Wolds was sealed off from the world. The gates were locked and guarded, telephones cut off, the crews prisoners.

Adam lit a cigarette, inhaled slowly. Leaving it so late to scrub the op was a mistake. It would have been better to unleash the Lancaster Force, regardless. Better by far. Nothing was more demoralising than going through the whole dreadful rigmarole of preparing for an op only to have the rug pulled from beneath your feet moments before the off.

He wondered what thoughts must be going through Eleanor's head, hearing the Halifaxes droning out to sea, reflecting on another lost Thursday. Another evening stolen by the vagaries of the war. Reluctantly, he turned his thoughts away from Eleanor.

The opening rounds of what the papers were calling 'the Berlin Blitz' could be chalked down in Bomber Command's favour. The weather, tactical innovation and outright, almost outrageous good fortune had kept losses down and seen untold mayhem sown in the streets of the Big City. Some of his sprogs were asking what all the fuss was about. Berlin had turned out to be a piece of cake. Granted, the flak was pretty fierce and the city was a long, long way away but they had braced themselves for something altogether bloodier and deadlier.

If his sprogs chose to regard Berlin as just another target, so be it. Long may they believe it. The fact of the matter was that thus far the weather had frustrated the defenders and sooner or later, they would surely have their revenge.

Pray God it was later...

Chapter 23

Thursday 25th November, 1943
The Gatekeeper's Lodge, Ansham Wolds, Lincolnshire

Eleanor sat at the kitchen table listening to the bombers climbing over Lincolnshire. In the parlour Kate McDonald was reading to Jonathan. Emmy was already in bed.

Kate had relaxed when Eleanor confirmed that not a single aircraft had taken off from Ansham Wolds that evening. The girl was happier, quietly optimistic now that she had spent a little time with her husband. There was a glow in her cheeks, and hope again in her bright young eyes.

"I wish I didn't have to go back tomorrow," she had told Eleanor. "I could stay a little longer, but Mac worries about me. I shouldn't have come down, he was right."

"But it's been lovely seeing each other?"

Kate had smiled happily, radiantly.

"Mac's applied for Pathfinders." She announced, proudly. Eleanor had raised an eyebrow and tried to veil her misgivings.

"Oh, really?" She understood that tours of duty with the Pathfinders were forty-five rather than the thirty operations flown elsewhere in Bomber Command.

"Wing-Commander Chantrey won't let him go, though."

"Oh." Eleanor wondered if she ought to be hearing this. Any of it.

"He said he needed Mac at Ansham Wolds and he wasn't having him 'swanning' off to Eight Group!"

"I see. So Mac's not going to join the Pathfinders, then?"

"No," Kate confirmed. "He's withdrawn his application."

Eleanor offered no comment. A transfer to the Pathfinder Force carried with it an automatic temporary promotion and a great deal of kudos. Had Mac wished he could have pressed matters further, and gone over his commanding officer's head.

Kate would be on her way first thing in the morning and it was unlikely she would see her husband again before she left. In the last week she had spent one afternoon and parts of two evenings with Mac. The rest of the time the RAF had kept him from her. Yet she was neither bitter, nor overly disappointed. She had come down to Lincolnshire to snatch a few hours with the man she loved and now that she had done so she was returning home stronger, and better able to face the future. Eleanor admired her stoicism.

While Kate was reading to Johnny from *The Wind in the Willows*, Eleanor had taken the opportunity to excuse herself so she could re-read the letter she had received that morning from her father. The numbness had been with her all day. It had clung to her like a shroud, distracting her every thought.

My Dear Eleanor,
In my life I have kept too many secrets

and told far too many lies - albeit mostly small white lies but lies nonetheless - to protect those secrets. I fear that I have become the prisoner of those secrets. Whilst discretion has always been the watchword in my work because secrets, and consequently, men's lives have rested in my hands, I have often been "discreet" to the point of being overly guarded in my relations with the people closest to me.

When I visited you last month I intended - in all honesty - to speak to you about many things. Things that I ought to have talked to you about long, long ago. But when it came to it my chains rattled and I honestly didn't know what to say. I had hoped also to make my peace with Adam Chantrey and as chance would have it I had the perfect opportunity to do just that at Bawtry Hall, but I fluffed my lines and missed my chance. In fact, I made a complete hash of it and I needlessly antagonised the boy.

Forgive me; I am beating about the bush. It is the habit of a lifetime for I have become a professional dissembler.

Let me come to the nub of things.

As you know, I have not been well since the spring. I told you that I had had a stroke, a small one, and that I was on the mend. This was not in fact the truth. My doctors have diagnosed a cancer and there is nothing they can do about it. They think I might have a month or two left (although, like all doctors, they can't agree amongst themselves). A month or two is the consensus but who knows?

There. I have admitted it! Please forgive me for not having the courage to tell you face to face.

I propose to decamp to your Aunt Lillian's house in Wimbledon later this week. I am not too steady on my pins and rather liable to take a spill if I am not very careful. In the circumstances, it seems wise to accept Lillian's long-standing invitation. You must not worry about me because I shall be in good hands. In a funny sort of way I am happier now than I have been for many years. I miss your dear mother terribly, and there is something very comforting about the thought that soon, I shall be joining her.

Now, to practical matters. Lillian will make whatever arrangements are necessary in due course. She has a copy of my Will, and another copy is lodged with my solicitors, Googe & Moresby. Latterly, I have taken the appropriate steps to ensure that my affairs are in good order. My estate goes to you and David, with David's half to be held in trust by Googe & Moresby pending his return from Germany.

About the houses. I have spoken to Messrs Googe & Moresby about this, but I strongly suggest you hang onto Heathcote Place and the town house in Oxford until after the war. There are people who say the war could go on for years and years, personally, I doubt it. The end is in sight, thank God. Another year, perhaps two at most and it will be over. I firmly believe the bombing this winter will go a long way to speeding the end and when our armies return to France, as they must next year, the Germans will not be able to hold out indefinitely.

What I am trying to say is that after the war property will be in short supply and that the houses will be worth a great deal more than they are presently. If you chose to send Jonathan to my old school, Harrow (or wherever, I know you have decidedly egalitarian views on these things) anything extra you can realise on the houses will be very handy. Likewise, the longer you hang onto the Gilts and War Bonds I have acquired, the better the return will be. In the past I have always found Edward Googe's advice in these matters sound.

I think that's enough about practicalities. You know your own mind, you always have. Just like your mother. But I've said what I wanted to say on these matters, anyway.

I know how difficult it is to travel these days and I don't expect you to come rushing down to be at my bedside. Perish the thought. You have the children to look after and responsibilities in Ansham Wolds. You've made a new life for yourself in Lincolnshire and I am proud of you. Lillian will look after me. Moreover, I recall how profoundly upsetting it was to watch your mother fade away and I don't want you to remember me that way. So please don't come down to Wimbledon. I am not being strong; it is just that I think it is best that things take their natural course. If there was some hope then perhaps I would feel differently, but there is no hope so I think the thing to do is accept the fact, and for you to get on with your life.

Now then, other matters: Adam Chantrey is a fine fellow. I say this because I suspect, and I shall feel extremely foolish if my imagination is playing tricks on me, that you are more than somewhat fond of young Chantrey. I never told you about the letter he wrote to me when David went missing. This was some while before we found out David was still alive. He wrote me a long, hand-written letter the day after the Wismar Raid in which he told me all about his time flying with David, and what an excellent, brave and decent chap David was. He described several of the ops David had flown, what a fine pilot he was and how his crew were devoted to him. He was describing a David I had never known, somebody who was responsible and grown up and making his own way in the world.

I ought to have shown you the letter. It was not the normal CO's form letter to next-of-kin, it was one of David's closest friends mourning his loss. He also told me that no aircraft had been seen to crash that night, so there was hope that David's Lancaster had ditched or landed somewhere, and that he might yet be safe. It made an immense impression on me at the time. I never showed you the letter because I thought it was best to keep the news that David was missing from you until we knew whether he was still alive. In the event of course, about a month later we heard David was in hospital in Germany.

I digress. Adam Chantrey. I know that my "approval" in these things is by and large, immaterial, but for what it is worth I do wholeheartedly and without reservation, "approve" of him. Assuming, that is, my guess about you two is correct, and I hope it is.

Again, you probably don't want my advice but I shall give it to you anyway. The only reckless thing I have done in my whole life was to marry your mother, bless her. I never regretted it. So, if you love him you must marry him.

All my love, Father

"Are you all right, Ellie?" Kate McDonald asked, standing in the doorway. Eleanor folded the sheets, stuffed them back into the envelope. She sniffed back a tear, forced a smile. She wondered how long the girl had been watching her.

"Yes. I'm fine."

"I thought you might have had some bad news, that's all?"

"My father's not very well."

"Oh. I'm sorry."

Chapter 24

Friday 26th November, 1943
RAF Ansham Wolds, Lincolnshire

Dusk was settling mistily over the high wold and the song of Merlins filled the air as Adam clambered out of the Bentley and pulled on his sheepskin flying jacket.

Ben Hardiman half-turned.

"Nice night for it," he observed, wryly.

"Good thing we weren't on for last night, what?"

"Low blow, skipper," his friend complained.

Barney Knight's R-Robert was lining up for takeoff in the middle distance, the pitch of her outer Merlins rising and falling as she manoeuvred into position. Behind R-Robert the rest of the Squadron's Lancasters rumbled around the perimeter road. The heartbeat of four score Merlins reverberated across the airfield.

Adam chuckled, mostly to himself.

Barney had – somewhat sheepishly - filled him in on the salient details of Wednesday night's sortie into Lincoln. Most of the Squadron's old lags had participated in the party, called ostensibly to celebrate the forthcoming transfer of several of their number to the newly created C Flight. Barney had been the Master of Ceremonies, and Ben his chief lieutenant as the gaggle of old lags navigated erratically from public house to public house. Late in the proceedings the local constabulary had made an ill-advised intervention. Outnumbered, more than one Constable had lost his trousers to concerted de-bagging exercises before reinforcements arrived to spoil the party. Thereafter, the hardest cases, Barney's crew, Ferris, Barlow, Ben and Jack Gordon had fetched up at the door of the Hare and Hounds in Kingston Magna. Other survivors, evaders and walking-wounded had dribbled back to the station throughout the small hours. At breakfast Peter Tilliard had had Jack Gordon carried into the Mess - trouser less and still very much the worse for wear - to have the handcuffs ceremonially sawn off his ankles amid a deafening chorus of hoots and cheers.

That morning Adam had despatched Tom Villiers to extricate the last few stragglers from the cells of Lincoln Police Station, a delicate task accomplished only after the Adjutant had provided a solemn undertaking that, 647 Squadron would reimburse the full cost of any police equipment and clothing damaged as a result of the night's operations out of Mess funds.

'Things got a bit out of hand, then?' Adam had inquired of Barney, when forewarned by Tom Villiers that the Lincoln constabulary had detained several of his old lags.

His second-in-command had blinked apologetically at him through bloodshot, puffy eyes.

'Just a tad, sir.'

'I thought the handcuffs were a nice touch.'

'Thank you, sir. I thought so, too. Some of the chaps thought Jack had it coming to him.'

Somehow, Ben Hardiman had contrived to effect a partial reconciliation between most of Barney's old lags and the rambunctious Australian navigator. The loud good humour with which Jack Gordon had borne the 'handcuffs incident' had gone a long way to cement that reconciliation.

'The police aren't overly impressed,' Adam had reminded his second in command.

'Miserable beggars in a reserved occupation!'

'No sense of humour,' Adam agreed. 'When Tom brings back the bill, make sure you put me down for a tenner.'

Barney had perked up at this.

'I say, sir. That's jolly decent of you.'

'Worth every penny,' Adam had assured him. 647 Squadron was building a reputation for pressing on and for hard-partying like judgement day was nigh. *Esprit de corps.* He wanted everybody else in 1 Group to hear about the legends and myths *his* crews were making up here on the High Wold, hoping and praying that the exploits of *his* crews would be remembered long after they were gone. He was proud of *his* men; as proud of the greenest sprog newly arrived from his OTU as he was of his oldest, most hard-bitten old lag. They were brothers one and all in the great crusade to save enough of the old world so that a new, better one might be built on whatever foundations survived. 'Worth every penny, Barney!'

Nearly every man involved in the Lincoln sortie had been listed to fly the previous night's cancelled Berlin op and many of them were flying tonight. There was nothing like a *Goodwood* to chase away a man's hangover. When, earlier that afternoon the curtain was removed to reveal the target, the groan in the Briefing Hall had been more than usually heartfelt.

R-Robert was rolling.

Tonight's operation was a variation of Thursday evening's cancelled plan: Lancaster Force to Berlin; Halifaxes to Stuttgart. This time the Chief had forsaken the direct route across northern Germany, electing to send both bomber forces across France, Belgium and the Rhineland to a position some thirty miles north-north-west of Frankfurt-am-Main. At this point the Halifaxes would break south and head for Stuttgart, and the Lancasters turn north-east for the Big City. Over Berlin the Pathfinders would replicate the tactics which had worked so well in the two previous attacks on the city. Special Blind Markers equipped with 3-centimetre *H2S* sets would drop yellow TIs and normal Blind Markers would put down red TIs. Other Pathfinder aircraft would continually refresh the initial marking pattern with green TIs. If at any stage the target was obscured by cloud or by smoke the Pathfinders would liberally sprinkle Sky Markers across the target area.

647 Squadron's Lancasters were carrying maximum fuel loads and a bomb load of 9,600 pounds. To accommodate this, the authorised take-off weights of his aircraft had been increased to 66,500 pounds.

Much to everybody's surprise the incremental raising of take-off weights had not resulted in the anticipated rash of accidents. Pragmatically, Adam assumed that Group would continue to gradually load more fuel and bombs onto its aircraft until such time as the accident rate indicated an appropriate operational limit had been reached.

R-Robert gathered speed. The end of the

runway was hidden by the mist. The Met Officer had promised Adam that the conditions would improve before the first of his heavies returned. He hoped so, presently, the fog was thickening over the wold. R-Robert's tail lifted off the clammy tarmac.

Barney did not know that this was his farewell op with 647 Squadron. Effective as of midnight he was grounded pending posting in command of his own squadron. Adam planned to break the news when he got back.

That afternoon Adam had asked his second in command to conduct the main crew briefing.

'Right chaps,' Barney had concluded. 'I don't want any of you beggars on the road until I've got to the front of the queue. RHIP's the ticket. Rank hath its privileges and I'm going to be the first off tonight. Woe betide any sprog who gets in my way!'

Barney Knight would do a good job wherever the AOC sent him.

R-Robert's navigation lights lifted into the mist, winked out in a moment. Already, the next Lancaster, A-Apple, was rolling. Behind A-Apple, K-King halted at the threshold. Her pilot gunned the throttles against the brakes, throttled back, watched the aircraft up ahead hurtle headlong into the deepening murk. High intensity goose-necked flares blazed dimly in the mist where the normal flare path lights disappeared into the night half-way down the runway.

"It's getting a bit dicey," Ben remarked, conversationally.

"It's okay at the moment," Adam returned, in a similar vein. Conditions were rapidly deteriorating towards the point where pilots could no longer distinguish the horizon. If it got much worse he would have to call a halt to take-offs.

Ben peered into the gloom. He knew what was going through his friend's mind. On other stations takeoffs would already have been suspended but this was not *any other* station. This was Ansham Wolds, high on the wold and plagued by low cloud at the best of times.

"Probably just us and Elsham Wolds who've got the problem."

"Probably."

One by one the Squadron's Lancasters roared into the fog as night fell over Lincolnshire.

N-Nan lined-up for takeoff.

Her sprog pilot cautiously advanced the throttles to zero boost against the brakes. Normally, a pilot throttled back almost immediately. The throttles either responded evenly or they did not. However, N-Nan's pilot held the throttles open for several seconds as if he was rechecking the gauges before throttling back, slowly, tentatively.

Adam stiffened, strained to listen to the beat of N-Nan's engines. His ear, keenly attuned to the thunder of Merlins, detected nothing immediately untoward. Perhaps, N-Nan's pilot was just nervous. There was a cheer from the big, noisy crowd of well-wishers: N-Nan was rolling. He listened harder as the bomber's Merlins raced. The bellow of her engines rose to a crescendo as the Lancaster swept past.

Something was wrong. Very wrong.

G-George was already lining up for takeoff.

Adam broke into a run towards the controller's Bedford lorry.

"Fire wagons!" He shouted through the open door. "FIRE WAGONS! NOW! NOW! NOW!"

Not pausing to wait for an acknowledgement he dived into the Bentley. Ben did likewise. He had no idea what was wrong but it never crossed his mind to question the fact that something was wrong. Very, very wrong. Adam gunned the Bentley's motor as the big man threw himself into the passenger seat. The car skidded into the night.

"N-Nan's losing power on one of her port Merlins!"

Ben did not ask him how knew. It was enough that he knew.

The bomber's navigation lights had disappeared into the fog.

N-Nan never got off the ground. Half-way down the runway her port outer Merlin misfired. There was a puff of smoke, evil blue-grey. The flash of flame, crimson red blazed a brief hole through the mist with sufficient ferocity to be visible across the whole aerodrome. The Merlin seized. With the throttle hard up against the stops the revs suddenly died and the Lancaster slewed off the centreline of the runway. Panic-stricken, her twenty-one year old sprog pilot wrestled the controls to hold the aircraft on the tarmac and off the sodden infield. At a hundred miles an hour and with the runway's foggy end rushing at him the gloom, N-Nan's pilot did the only thing he could do. He forced the throttles through the gate, screamed for maximum boost and tried to get the bomber into the air. It was too late to abort the take off.

With her tanks topped up to the brim and over four tons of bombs stashed in her cavernous bomb bay N-Nan was too heavy to take off on three engines.

She ploughed off the end of the runway, smashed through the perimeter fence and into the field beyond, swinging to the right. Trees reared up out of the mist, standing proud either side of the deep culvert that drained the surrounding fields into the Ansham Brook. N-Nan's wheels sank into the soft earth, her undercarriage collapsed, and flew into countless fragments. Her propellers, spinning at thousands of revolutions per minute struck ground and stopped in a fraction of a second. The raging Merlins tore themselves to pieces. The Lancaster squashed down into the mud, gouging a deep, jagged furrow in the field, sliding, slipping towards the trees. Even though the mire slowed her headlong rush she shouldered into the wood line with a rending, jarring impact. The port wing was ripped off, and the rest of the wreck slithered to a halt in the culvert, the starboard wing tip jutting skyward at an angle of forty-five degrees.

The fire engines raced across the infield. Ambulances rushed from their holding position behind the distant watchtower. Adam hurled the Bentley into the fog. As the car jolted and skidded over the turf a great, black shape roared past in the darkness.

G-George surging down the runway.

Crash or no crash as long as the runway remained unobstructed it was the controller's job to ensure that takeoffs continued. Adam's standing orders on this, and other ops-related matters, were explicit.

He swerved to overtake a fire engine that had been placed near the end of the runway.

N-Nan was already on fire. Burning fuel spilled into the culvert. The bomber's tail was cocked up into the air, silhouetted against the flames. Burning 100-octane flowed down the culvert towards the Ansham Brook far below, a ribbon of fire in the fog.

The Bentley slid to a stop inches from the gaping hole in the fence. The wreck was about seventy or eighty yards beyond the perimeter. Another heavy lifted into the night, clawed for height, her Merlins bellowing in protest. N-Nan's incendiaries were sparking into life, glowing an evil blue-white on the ground all around the crash and inside the ruptured, broken-backed carcass of the Lancaster.

Adam jumped out and unthinkingly, ran full tilt towards N-Nan. A wing tank suddenly ignited, flames flared fifty feet in the air. The heat reached out, brushed Adam's face. He heard a warning shout.

"She's going to blow up!"

The mud underfoot slowed him, sucked at his running feet. He ran on a dozen paces, it was like running through treacle. There was another warning shout, this time louder, closer, and much more insistent.

"GET DOWN, YOU IDIOT!"

Adam ignored it. He had to get to N-Nan.

The next thing he knew he was rugby tackled from behind. A diving shoulder took him at waist height, knocked the breath out of his lungs. Strong arms encircled him, dumped him on the ground, pinning him down.

A split second later N-Nan's cookie erupted.

The earth convulsed, the blast wave washed overhead. Adam threw his arms in front of his face. All around him mud, shrapnel and blazing stick incendiaries rained down. Distantly, another Lancaster was taking off. It flew over the perimeter fence, climbing by the light of hundreds of fizzing, glowing, smoking, sparking incendiaries.

Slowly, Adam sat up, looked dazedly at Ben.

The big man grinned sheepishly.

"Sorry," he shrugged.

"Not at all, old man," Adam muttered. His ears were ringing and sound was registering distantly as if through a pillow. He searched for his muddy cap, jammed it on his head. His ears were ringing. Ben had probably just saved his life. Running full pelt towards seven tons of burning 100-octane and over four tons of high explosives was not the cleverest thing he had done that day. He had got a bit carried away in the heat of the moment. Everybody was entitled to an aberration every now and again. "I suppose on balance," he admitted. "Trying to put out the fire with my bare hands wasn't the best possible plan."

The two men got to their feet. They were both covered in mud. Around them incendiaries spluttered in the wet earth, lacing the air with acrid phosphorus and magnesium fumes. Adam and Ben looked at each other. In the flickering, blue-white light they looked every inch like escaped lunatics.

"No," the big man agreed. "But it's always good to have a plan."

Trudging back to the perimeter fence firemen ran past them in the opposite direction. Above them Lancasters clawed for height over Lincolnshire, set their courses into the south and the distant convergence point, mid-way between Brighton and Abbeville.

"How did you know Nan was about to crash, Skipper?"

"The silly sod oiled up the plugs on his port outer Merlin," Adam retorted, irritably. "He saw the drop on the gauge but ignored it. Either that or he thought he'd done something to oil up the plugs when there was actually a genuine mechanical problem with the engine."

"Oh. Not clever."

"No. Not clever."

Chapter 25

Friday 26th November, 1943
The Rectory, Ansham Wolds, Lincolnshire

The Rectory was more than a mile from the crash site but the flash of the huge explosion momentarily lit up the kitchen through the blackout drapes. Startled, the plate she was drying slipped from Eleanor's hands. It fell on the stone floor and shattered loudly. Simultaneously, the windows rattled and a second later the dull, rumbling crump of the detonation rolled down the valley like a nearby thunderclap.

"My goodness!" Exclaimed the Reverend Naismith-Parry, emerging from his study. "What on earth was that?"

"I think it came from on top of the Wold," Eleanor gasped, recovering a little of her equilibrium. "From the fields behind Ansham Hall. At the end of the runway." A fully laden Lancaster must have crashed on takeoff. "Oh, dear," she murmured, realising she was treading on broken crockery. "I seem to have, er…"

The Rector was taken aback to see Eleanor so completely distracted, helpless. He stepped over the shards of china on the kitchen floor, took the woman's arm, and drew her into the parlour.

"Come and sit down, my dear," he soothed, gently, paternally, sitting her in an armchair.

"Simon, you must make sure Adelaide is all right."

"In due course, my dear."

The Rector's wife had taken to her bed earlier that day with a head cold. For the moment the Reverend Naismith-Parry was more concerned about Eleanor. Only that afternoon she had told him about her father's letter. The contents of that letter, added to Johnny's bouts of quarrelsomeness and the fast approaching humiliation of being unjustly hauled before the local Justices over Edward Rowbotham's trifling - most likely trumped up breaches of the blackout regulations - had, briefly, begun to prey on her mind. She had poured out her troubles. The Rector had listened quietly, sympathetically; tried to reassure her. Johnny would grow out of his tantrums. The business over the blackout regulations was a disgrace, it was high time he had a stiff word with Edward Rowbotham.

'I'm sure your father is trying to be kind. Making the best of a difficult situation.' Understandably, Eleanor was desperately worried, desolate. Not at all her normal optimistic, resilient self.

'It's not just that I feel I ought to be doing more,' she had explained, biting her lip unconsciously. 'I really want to do more. Oh, I wish father had been sensible and talked to me when he was up here last month. I could have done something then. I could have made arrangements to nurse him myself. I've thought about going down to Wimbledon to help Aunt Lillian, but she and I have never hit it off and besides, there are the children to think of. And the school. And Adelaide's not been well. I can't just drop everything and go down to Wimbledon. I don't know what to do, Simon? Even if I could persuade father to stay with me, how on earth would he get here? What can I do?'

And *now* a Lancaster had crashed and blown up.

Inevitably, she was fretting about Adam Chantrey.

"I'm sorry, Simon," Eleanor sighed. "I seem to be going to pieces at the moment."

The old man smiled. "It's quite natural that you should be upset, and worried. You've had a bad knock. You can't be strong all the time."

"I'm hardly ever strong!" She exclaimed. "Most of the time it's an act."

"Well," said the Rector. "If it is an act, it's a very good one, my dear."

"You're very sweet to say so." Eleanor was close to tears, thankful that her children had gone to supper with the Bowmans that evening. The Publican of the Sherwood Arms and his wife were currently fostering a brood of four evacuees from Sheffield, aged five to eight. The Bowman's had no children of their own, something that Eleanor suspected caused them immense regret.

There were those in the village who discouraged contact between their children and the Bowman's evacuees, Eleanor thought this was odd. The last thing she wanted was for her son and daughter to grow up sheltered from the realities of the world.

Lancasters were taking off in the night. One of their number had crashed but the rest were pressing on. Eleanor shivered.

"Father says I should marry Adam," she blurted, out of the blue. "What do you think, Simon?"

The Reverend Naismith-Parry made every

appearance of taking this in his stride. He did not bat an eyelid. Inwardly, alarm bells rang. For all they knew the crash on the hill above the village was the dashing Wing-Commander's funeral pyre.

"Do you love him?"

Eleanor nodded, in tears.

"Oh, yes. Very much."

"Well then?" The Rector and his wife had guessed as much from the beginning, rejoiced for her.

Eleanor looked up into the old man's face. "Not that he's asked me to marry him," she went on. "He might not. He's got so many other things to think about, of course. So many other things..."

The Rector refused to be deflected by this.

"But if he did ask you to marry him," he prompted. "Would you?"

Eleanor dabbed her eyes with a dainty, lace handkerchief. She blew her nose, sniffed back her tears, forced a smile. A defiant, brave smile.

"Of course I would."

Chapter 26

Friday 26th November, 1943
RAF Ansham Wolds, Lincolnshire

Miraculously, all seven members of N-Nan's sprog crew had escaped the crash with nothing worse than a wide and varied assortment of cracked ribs, bloody but essentially superficial lacerations and numerous bone deep bruises. The moment the aircraft had come to a halt they had jumped out and run for their lives with the electric alacrity of young men who had believed they were about to be imminently burned alive.

It seemed that the only man at Ansham Wolds who had been so stupid as to actually sprint *towards* the burning bomber was their CO. Whom, all things being equal, ought to have known better.

"Well, what happened, Morris?" Adam inquired gruffly, stepping into the ambulance. Ben had taken him by the elbow and virtually frog-marched him – several times - around the vehicle before allowing him anywhere near N-Nan's sprogs. The big man had barred his way, looked him straight in the eye like only a friend could. If it had come to it he would have rugby tackled him a second time. It was by no means the first time Ben had saved Adam - when his blood was up - from making a complete ass of himself.

Recognising the mud-spattered newcomer, Sergeant Pilot Morris tried to stand up. The WAAF trying to staunch the flow of blood from an ugly gash on his forehead put a hand on his shoulder and restrained him.

"For goodness sake! We're not standing on ceremony here!" Adam snapped, exasperated. "Sit down, man!"

The boy was shaking like a leaf. He was terrified of his CO, anyway. Sprogs tended to be. To them the legendary Wingco was a half-man, half-myth. Confronting a living legend was bad enough, confronting him when one had just made an incredibly bad mistake was the boy's worst nightmare.

"Spit it out. What happened?"

"We had a bit of mag drop on the port outer, sir," stuttered the young Welshman. "Borderline, like, sir. Didn't reckon much on it. Thinking about it now I maybe oiled up the plugs, accidentally like, sir. Anyway, it seemed okay until we were about half way down the runway. Then, all of a sudden there was a misfire, a big bang and the revs fell off. The kite tried to step sideways, like. By the time I'd got her straight again it was too late to abort. Trouble was, what with the kite being so heavy, she wouldn't unstick on three engines, sir."

Adam scowled. The boy would have done better to chop back on the throttles and let the Lancaster drift off the runway and onto the infield. Better to risk a ground loop than to barrel into the perimeter fence at a hundred knots. These and other matters would be discussed with Sergeant Pilot Morris in the morning. The boy deserved a fair hearing. A fair hearing and an exemplary, just punishment.

"I see," Adam ground out. The ambulance bumped and swayed along the runway. Two other members of N-Nan's crew sat battered, bloodied and dejected in the back of the vehicle. There was an awkward silence. He relented. Sighed deeply, shook his head. "Has anybody got a cigarette?"

His cigarette case was in the Bentley, which Ben had promised to drive back to the Briefing Hall. One of N-Nan's gunners produced a crumpled pack. They all lit up. The sprogs had had a bad experience, a nasty scare. They were shaken up, down in the mouth. This was not the time to rub further salt into their wounds.

Adam sniffed, rubbed his muddy chin.

"Cheer up, chaps. Take it from me if you can walk away from a crash like that the rest of your tour is going to be a piece of cake!"

"Good lord!" Exclaimed Group Captain Alexander, catching sight of his Wing-Commander's dishevelment as he jumped down from the ambulance. "Whatever happened to you?"

"Tad too close to N-Nan when her cookie lit up, sir."

"Oh, I see. I gather all the chaps are accounted for?"

"Yes, sir."

"That's something I suppose." They set off towards the administration hut.

Adam checked they were out of earshot of any member of the gaggle of sightseers who had surrounded the ambulance.

"Sergeant Pilot Morris disregarded a mag drop. He thought he'd inadvertently oiled up the plugs when in fact he probably had a serious engine problem," he reported, sarcastically. "For reasons best known to himself the silly little sod then proceeded to try to take off."

"Press on spirit, what!" Remarked the Old Man, his tone almost cheerful. "Never mind, look on the bright side."

"I wasn't aware there was a bright side, sir?"

The Group Captain laughed.

"At least he didn't block the runway, what!"

Adam's sense of humour had temporarily gone missing in action. Excusing himself he hurried to his quarters to wash, brush up and don clean battledress. His batman, Crawford magically materialised within moments of his unexpected return to his billet.

"Crawford, you're supposed to be off duty," Adam upbraided him mildly.

"A gentleman's gentleman is never off duty, sir," replied the unflappable Crawford.

"You're not a gentleman's gentleman, you're my batman!"

"Yes, sir," acknowledged the older man, retrieving a freshly pressed tunic from the rickety wardrobe at the foot of the cot. "Whatever you say, sir. Batman it is, sir."

Adam smiled. His smile soon faded. Outside the fog was thickening by the minute. It swirled in dank, impenetrable clouds across the airfield, and settled coldly, evilly on the ground.

"Where's the bloody Met Officer?" He barked, stalking into the Operations Room. "Find him!"

He dumped himself on a chair in the small, cramped alcove that served as the Intelligence Officer's den. The fog was supposed to be clearing. Instead it was clamping down for the night. A real pea-souper. If it got any worse a chap would hardly be able to see his hand in front of his face. His

Lancasters could not land in this. Nobody's Lancs could land in this. He lit a cigarette, brooded on the fog.

Presently, the voice of Flight-Lieutenant the Reverend Poore intruded into his thoughts.

"Ah, Wing-Commander."

"Hello, Padre," Adam groaned. His ears still rang but his hearing was otherwise returning to normal. "What can I do for you?"

"I, er, looked in at the dispensary," he reported. "The Flight Surgeon was attending to those poor boys."

Adam felt that this was an opportune moment to correct the Reverend Poore on a matter of technical detail.

He coughed. "*Sprogs*, Padre."

"I'm sorry?"

"*Sprogs*, Padre," he repeated, brusquely. "Those 'poor boys' are 'sprogs' who have just perpetrated an avoidable accident and occasioned the loss of a valuable aircraft. They're bloody lucky to be alive. However, by the time I've finished with them they'll probably wish they weren't!"

"Oh, I see. I hadn't looked at it like that." The Padre's earnestness was more than a little comical. "Actually, I half expected to find you in the hospital. I gather you were, er, as close as anybody to the explosion."

"I hit the deck before the big bang."

"Very wise, I'm sure, sir."

"That's a good tip for the future, Padre," Adam went on, grimly. "The next time an aircraft blows up, remember to hit the deck. Pronto! Okay?"

"I shall try to remember that, sir," the Padre

replied. "The next time."

The younger man could not tell whether the cleric was being serious or not.

"You do!"

The Reverend Poore pursed his lips, glanced over his shoulder.

"I never realised our, er, cookies, were that powerful, that awesome," he said, quietly. The immense, fiery bloom of the great white detonation had left him deeply shocked. The carnage such weapons - dropped in their hundreds - must wreak in densely packed city streets hardly bore contemplation. "I never realised."

No," Adam sighed. "People don't, Padre."

Chapter 27

Saturday 27th November, 1943
RAF Ansham Wolds, Lincolnshire

By midnight fog extended across Lincolnshire and the Fens, blanketing the fields of 1 and 5 Group's Lancasters. The order to divert the returning heavies north of the Humber to the Yorkshire stations of 4 and 6 Group's Halifaxes was broadcast. In Yorkshire, where the fog was only a little less impenetrable, the bases braced themselves for the worst and the worst was not long delayed. By one in the morning Lancasters were crashing and men were dying in the fog.

The skies over the Big City had been relatively clear and the searchlights, the flak and the fighters had given the bomber stream a tempestuous ride as it traversed the city. For the sprogs who had come to regard the Berlin flak as 'a piece of cake' in earlier raids, the terrible dazzle of the searchlights and the unrelenting ferocity of the barrage was a horribly rude awakening. The trial by fire had claimed at least a dozen victims over the target.

Notwithstanding the absence of cloud it was likely the Pathfinders had put their initial marking pattern down several miles north of the intended aiming point in the centre of Berlin. Against any other German city this would have condemned the operation to abject failure. Over the Big City, it simply meant that the main weight of the attack had fallen on the 'wrong' part of the city: specifically, the industrialised north-western sector, on the Reinickendorf, Tegel, Wittenau and Siemensstadt districts. Over three hundred cookies and as many as three hundred thousand stick incendiaries had gone down into the rubble-strewn suburbs of the north-west, west and central areas of the German capital.

After the attack strong winds had dispersed the returning bombers, driven the unwary off track and to their doom. Then, over England, exhausted crews, some nursing damaged aircraft, all running low on fuel found themselves forced to divert to unfamiliar, distant airfields by the fog. Over Yorkshire the returning bombers circled in droves while on the ground the nightmare grew apace. There were too many aircraft and only a handful of 4 and 6 Group's fields were wholly fog-free. The men in the Lancasters stacked over northern England watched their fuel burn up and the mist spread across the ground. The Yorkshire bases were overwhelmed. Airfield after airfield had to turn away aircraft, their runways blocked by crashes. Within an hour a score of aircraft had crash-landed, or simply crashed.

By daylight the provisional butcher's bill read: 28 Lancasters missing in action, another 15 written off or destroyed in crashes in England, and as many again seriously damaged. At a stroke ten percent of the Lancaster Force had been wiped off the order of battle. 647 Squadron had lost two aircraft: K-King had flown into a low hill trying to land at Leeming, killing all onboard; and R-Robert with Barney Knight and his veteran crew was listed as missing.

Adam refused to accept the fact Barney was

gone at first but as the hours dragged by without word, the reality of it slowly sank in. By mid-morning there was no hope, no mistake, no doubt. Around nine o'clock he retreated to his office and shut the door. He chain-smoked, brooded, empty and lost until, at ten on the dot, there was a hesitant knock at his office door.

He started with alarm.

"Get a grip, man!" He hissed under his breath, realising he had been staring into nowhere for some minutes. He had not washed, or eaten. He was unshaven, his battledress crumpled. What sort of an example was that for *his* people? He clenched his fists, took a deep breath. "Get a grip, man!"

Three long, deepening breaths.

Then: "Come!"

Sergeant Pilot Morris limped into the room, half his head was swathed in bulky white bandages, his face puffy and mottled. He stood stiffly, painfully to attention before his CO's desk, braced to take his medicine.

"Sergeant Morris, reporting as ordered," he forced out, voice trembling. "Sir!"

Adam had forgotten all about N-Nan.

After what had happened in the small hours of the morning the events of the off seemed a very long time ago. He dimly recollected having instructed N-Nan's pilot to report to him at oh-ten hundred hours.

"Stand easy," he grated.

Morris stood at ease but did not relax. He stared directly to his front, swallowing nervously.

"Last night you tried to fly a Lanc to Berlin on three engines and a prayer. Whilst not wishing to decry, *per se*, the power of prayer, I trust that you are now fully apprised of its limitations, Sergeant?"

"Yes, sir." Morris was shaking like a leaf.

"Why on earth did you try and take off?"

"I didn't want to let the Squadron down, sir."

Adam despaired. How could he tear the boy off a strip? The young Welshman was self-evidently more afraid of him than he was of the enemy. And how on earth could he reprimand the boy for pressing on too much?

"Very commendable."

I didn't want to let the Squadron down.

"Will there be an inquiry, sir?"

Adam eyed the sprog bleakly.

"I don't think that will be necessary, Morris," he snapped acidly, coming to a decision. "We both know exactly what happened last night, do we not?"

"Yes, sir!"

"I expect my crews to press on, Morris. What you did last night wasn't pressing on, it was stupid. Bloody stupid! Do I make myself clear?"

N-Nan's pilot's head dropped perceptibly.

"Yes, sir."

Last night Adam would have happily crucified the boy but in the clear light of morning he knew he could not punish him, even though by the strict letter of the law he was duty bound to throw the book at him. The boy's heart was in the right place. That was what mattered; the only thing that mattered. The boy had made a mistake. Mistakes happened. Hopefully, he would learn from it. Morris and his crew were listed to transfer from B to C Flight. He would leave matters in Peter Tilliard's capable hands. Peter would have the young Welshman running engine checks until he was heartily sick of it, until he could cut the mustard blindfold.

"That will be all."

Sergeant Pilot Morris's mouth gaped open. His surprise was palpable, and in other circumstances would have been comical. The boy stared at his CO for a moment, rooted to the spot.

"I don't understand, sir?" He blurted. "You're not grounding me, sir?"

"No," Adam told him, tersely. "Everybody makes mistakes, Morris. The trick is not to repeat them. In your flight log you will record that your aircraft crashed on take-off due to an engine fire caused by an unspecified and unsuspected mechanical failure. You will bring that log to me and I will counter sign that entry. Thereafter, that will constitute the official verdict on last night's incident. As for an investigation..."

Adam allowed himself the luxury of a shrug.

"I witnessed the whole thing so there's no need for any further investigation. So far as I'm concerned the incident is closed. You are dismissed!"

The pilot snapped to attention, and not so much marched as sprinted out of the room.

Many moons ago, lumbering about the sky in a rattling, decrepit Blenheim night fighter Adam had come in to land at Tangmere. The night was dark, the sortie had been long and fruitless, contactless. Faraway, Portsmouth was burning. As he lined up on the flare path, applied maximum flap and juggled the throttles Ben had tapped him on the shoulder.

"Skipper!" The big man had bellowed in his ear, straining to overcome the racket of the engines.

"What?"

"I didn't feel the undercarriage lock down, Skipper!"

With a sinking feeling Adam had gunned the engines, climbed back into the circuit. On his second approach he had *remembered* to lower the landing gear.

"Much better with the wheels down," Ben had remarked, chortling, as they jumped down from the aircraft.

Nobody was perfect.

Barney Knight was gone and there were pieces to be picked up. Tonight there would be a party in the Mess. A hell of a party. Barney would have wanted that; it was fitting, only right and proper. But first there were arrangements to be made, letters to be written.

"Damned bad luck about young Knight," declared Group Captain Alexander sauntering into the office moments after Morris departed. "You sent Morris off with a flea in his earl, what?" He inquired, glancing over his shoulder.

"Yes, sir. I think Morris has learned his lesson."

"I jolly well hope so!" The older man was muffled in his greatcoat. He suggested: "A walk will do you a world of good."

They marched across the damp infield, Rufus loping in the near distance. The fog of the night before was lifting off the high wold and mocking rays of watery sunlight washed over the station.

"Knight's last trip with the Squadron, too. Damned shame."

"That's the way it goes," Adam rejoined softly.

Soon the first of the Squadron's Lancasters would be taking off from the over-crowded Yorkshire bases of 4 and 6 Groups.

The Lancaster Force had been stood down at first light. Even if the weather permitted, after last night's debacle there was no realistic possibility of mounting a major attack for forty-eight, perhaps seventy-two hours. Perhaps, longer. In addition to the crashed and damaged aircraft, many aircraft had been over-stressed, force-landed. Every bomber would need to be closely, minutely inspected.

"A lot of the chaps won't have heard about Barney, yet," Adam said. "Ben and Jack Gordon are organising a bash in the Mess for tonight."

"Ah, yes," Alexander grunted. "A good bash. Nothing like it. It's just what young Knight would have wanted." He glanced at his Wing-Commander. The boy was tired, withdrawn, a little preoccupied. All of which was entirely understandable. However, this morning he thought he detected something else. Something more than weariness. If it was any other man but Chantrey he would have suspected the young tyro was shaken, not at all himself. "Look, my boy," he advised, careful not to be heavy-handed. "It doesn't do to take things to heart."

"I didn't think I was, sir."

"Well, that's all right, then."

Adam locked away his inner turmoil. The knowledge that his mask had slipped and momentarily betrayed him granted him a second wind, and stiffened his determination to battle on.

"Barney must be replaced."

"Without delay," the Group Captain agreed. "I'll get on the line to Group, see what we can turn up, what?"

"I'd like to keep it in the family, sir."

"Oh. If you think it's for the best."

"I do, sir."

"Who, then?" They had halted, turned to face one another.

"Mick Ferris, sir."

Adam contemplated the Old Man's thinly veiled dismay over a cup of tea in his office that afternoon while he awaited the arrival of Flight-Lieutenant Michael Ferris, DFC. The Station Master had grounds for disquiet. Good grounds.

"You wanted to see me as soon as I got back, sir?" Ferris grinned. It took more than a mere overnight decimation of the Lancaster Force to dislodge the grin from Mick Ferris's face.

Adam waved the newcomer into the seat opposite his desk. His head ached from too many cigarettes, as it often did of late, and his mood was less than sanguine as he viewed the burly Ulsterman for a moment.

"Barney bought it last night, Mick."

Ferris had landed safely at Linton-on-Ouse at a little after two o'clock that morning. Nobody had told him the bad news in the short time since his return to Ansham Wolds. He was still decked out in his flying gear, having come straight from dispersals. The Ulsterman uttered an oath almost, but not quite under his breath. Barney had gathered about him a small circle of fiercely loyal old lags. Ferris had been his devoted right hand man, always in the thick of any scrap. Thirteen ops into his second Lancaster tour nobody could deny that Mick Ferris was a good man to have at your side in a fight. As witnessed by the fact he had a well-documented habit of blotting his copy book.

Ferris blinked at his CO, realisation dawning that somebody was going to have to fill Barney's shoes. *Him.* In his own way he was as dismayed by the thought as Group Captain Alexander had been earlier in the day. The Old man regarded Ferris as the Squadron's bane, a bad lot. However, from where Adam sat, Ferris was probably the *only* man for the job. Of all his old lags none was as bloody-minded or as convinced of his own invulnerability as Mick Ferris.

Adam dispensed with the niceties.

"Barney's gone and somebody's got to take his place. I've decided to give you the first crack at it." This said, he rose to his feet, stretched and went to the window, restless despite his tiredness.

Ferris remained seated, oddly poker-faced. He had had as little as possible to do with the Wingco, judged it the best policy. It paid to be wary of living legends and that, after all, was what the CO was. Chantrey was the sort of chap everybody had heard about and that everybody had a story about. Chantrey was one of 5 Group's Lancaster kings; the band of brothers whose number included the likes of John Nettleton, the man who had led 12 and 97 Squadrons in broad daylight to the MAN Works - Maschinenfabrik Augsburg-Nürnberg - at Augsburg, and Guy Gibson, CO of 617 Squadron, of 'Dambusters' fame. It was Bomber Command's most exclusive club and Adam Chantrey was a founder member. Membership of that club gave a man rights. So Ferris listened to his CO. And moreover, he listened attentively.

The Wingco was silhouetted in the window.

"I think you've got it in you to make a bloody good fist of it. It won't be easy. Barney's a hard act to follow."

Ferris cleared his throat.

"I don't know what to say, sir."

"Don't say anything, then!" Adam slumped back into his chair and dug out a cigarette. He tossed his silver cigarette case to Ferris, both men lit up. He leaned forward, fixed the Ulsterman with his gaze which today was steelier than ever. "You've got yourself a bit of a bad name," he said, matter of factly. "You don't like taking orders, you're insubordinate, you're a trouble-maker, and you're a damned sight too inclined to let your fists do the talking. A chap like you ought to have his own squadron by now. *My* Flight Commanders don't get into bar room brawls. It's just not done, Mick."

"Understood, sir."

Ferris saw the glint in his CO's eyes.

"I hope so, Mick. I hope so." Adam's temples throbbed unmercifully. His voice was low. "Old lags like us have a responsibility to the others. It's up to us to make sure the chaps get a fair crack of the whip. It doesn't matter how many ops a fellow's got under his belt. It's the example he sets that matters. It's high time you stopped acting like a damned fool, Mick. High time."

"Yes, sir."

Adam hoped the Ulsterman would take it to heart.

"Good." He allowed himself a thin, half-smile. "For Christ's sake don't make a hash of it, Mick."

Chapter 28

Saturday 27th November, 1943
The Gatekeeper's Lodge, Ansham Wolds, Lincolnshire

Eleanor had been unable to sleep. She had heard the aircraft landing at the airfield throughout the day, then when after dusk the skies had quietened, she had hoped that Adam would call. But he had neither called, nor sent her a message. Any message. For all she knew he might be dead.

No, not that.

Somebody would have told her if he was dead. Bad news always got through, travelled fast. Had something happened to Adam, Group Captain Alexander, perhaps Mac, or Tom Villiers, the Adjutant would have sent her word. Somebody would have told her.

It was nearly midnight. She had pulled a thick, woollen robe over her nightdress and wrapped a shawl about her shoulders, settled in the kitchen. The warmth of the range kept the cold at bay while she sat in an old pine rocking chair reading by the light of a single candle. Jane Austen's prose took her away from the realities of the world, immersed her in the idiosyncratic, closeted society of the gentlefolk of nineteenth century England. *Persuasion* was not her favourite Austen work - *Sense and Sensibility* and *Emma* vied for that distinction - but it was a book she returned to every few years, finding new, fresh things in it each time.

She heard the car in the lane, the muffled

squeal of brakes.

It was *him*. It could only be *him*. Eleanor put down her book, forgetting to mark the page. Shielding the candle she shuffled through the darkened parlour and swung open the door as the man was about to knock.

Adam was cap less, swaying. He staggered, leaned against the door frame, squinting at the woman in the dim, flickering light of the candle. He reeked of beer and cigarette smoke. He was obviously very drunk. Eleanor looked beyond him into the night, he was alone.

"You've been drinking," she said, both angry and relieved. Her anger evaporated into the night, relief washed over her.

"Afraid so," he slurred, proudly. His eyes were glazed, his legs unsteady, rubbery.

"How on earth did you drive here in the state you're in?" Eleanor demanded, whispering shrilly.

"Auto pilot, dear lady. Auto pilot. I say, did you know there was some ferret-faced chappie hiding in the hedge, I damned nearly almost collected him on the bonnet coming round the corner..."

Eleanor took his arm, pulled him inside.

"That will be the Chief ARP Warden, again," she sighed, ruefully, and quickly shut the door at his back. "The dreadful little man is always spying on me." Adam stumbled over the mat, suddenly pressed her against the wall. She gasped, winded, dropped her candle, pushed him away in the darkness.

"Sorry," he muttered, belching. He took a deep breath. "Bit worse for wear. Sorry. Bad day at the office..."

"Stay where you are, Adam!" Eleanor told him, adopting her sternest schoolmistress tone. "I'll light another candle. Don't you dare move an inch. Not one inch!"

"Right you are!"

"And try not to make such a row! You'll wake Johnny and Emmy!"

"Sorry..."

Eleanor went to the kitchen, located the matches and another candle, ready in its holder. She returned by the light of the new candle. Taking the man by the elbow she shepherded him through the parlour without incident, and into the kitchen.

"Sit down before you fall down, darling."

"Right..." He slumped into the chair by the table with a heartfelt sigh, staring at her unsteadily as she drew up another chair, joined him at the table. "Damn.... Shouldn't have come, not like this."

Eleanor had recovered her composure and was about to whisper reassurance when the man suddenly lurched to his feet.

"I think I'm going to throw up," he announced.

"This way!" Eleanor unbolted the door to the yard, unceremoniously shoved Adam on his way. Patiently, she listened while he was noisily, violently sick outside in the pitch blackness. Gradually, the retching slowed, stopped. The man groaned.

"Dreadfully sorry," he croaked, fighting for air. "Making a fool of myself, sorry."

"For goodness sake. Stop apologising."

"Sorry..." The man propped himself up against the wall of the yard. "You couldn't lend me a hand, could you?" He asked feebly. "Think I'm going to fall over..."

Eleanor half-carried, half-dragged him inside and dumped him back in the chair in front of the range. He had said 'a bad day at the office'. The words now sent a chill down her spine.

"Something has happened, hasn't it?" She asked, urgently.

Adam looked at her blankly. The woman's face drifted in and out of focus, the room rolled from side to side. His thoughts were confused, disordered, meandering. The evening was a blur of voices and faces, songs sung bawdily, lustily. He remembered Mick Ferris leading the Mess in song. They had sung the Eton Boating Song for Barney, and damned nearly brought down the roof! A bloody good bash, Barney would have enjoyed it. A bloody good bash. Just the ticket...

"What has happened?" Eleanor prompted, again. "Tell me what has happened?"

Now that his stomach was empty Adam felt a little less ill. He sobered somewhat, swallowed but the vile taste in his mouth persisted.

"Things," he sniffed. "Just things. Sorry. I ought to go. Making a fool of myself. Behaving like a damned fool..."

Eleanor reached out and put a hand on his shoulder.

"You stay where you are. I haven't got any coffee, so tea will have to do. You sit there while I make us a nice pot of tea. A nice *strong* pot of tea."

Her calming aura concentrated Adam's rambling, disjointed thoughts. He viewed her sheepishly, said nothing as she fed wood and shavings into the stove, filled the kettle from the big jug. Watching Eleanor move about the kitchen slowed his thoughts and temporarily distracted him from the events of the last day.

His mind wandered.

Living in the relative lap of luxury on RAF stations he had grown accustomed to having mains water on tap, electric light available at the press of a switch. Eleanor's cottage had none of these amenities. Water had to be drawn from the well, pumped up by hand. Lighting was by candles or oil lamps, heat came from the kitchen range and fires in open hearths. It was a salutary reminder that the modern age had yet to encompass much of the rural hinterland of Lincolnshire. Communities like Ansham Wolds had until recently existed much as they had done a hundred years ago. The canal and railway ages had passed the village by, and few of the material and technological advances of the twentieth century had manifested themselves in the day to day lives of the villagers. Then the war had come and with it the heavies of Bomber Command...

"Are you feeling a little better?"

Eleanor's question shattered his train of thought.

"A bit, thanks."

"Good." In the background the kettle was steaming. She paused to warm the pot, spooned tea from the caddy, poured hot water, let the pot stand a while and the leaves stew. They were silent. Presently, she placed a cup before the man. "Drink that."

He sipped his tea.

Eleanor brushed down her robe, drew her shawl close and joined the man at the table. She gazed at him by candlelight.

"I was up at the Rectory when the big explosion happened yesterday," she said, cautiously. "It was quite a shock."

Adam grimaced.

"One of my sprogs tried to take off on three engines and a prayer," he told her. "Ended up making a bloody great big hole in the perimeter fence at the end of the runway. And an even bigger one in the field the other side of it. No harm done. All the chaps baled out before the kite went up."

"Oh."

"Last night was a bit of a shambles all round, actually. Fog, you see. Bad medicine, fog. Main Force got diverted north of the Humber when it got back. Aircraft down all over the shop. One of my kites flew into a hill..."

Eleanor tried not to look too horrified. The man was drunk, his words slurred and laboured, his voice faltering. Not trusting herself to speak, she hid behind her tea cup.

"Only sprogs. But sprogs are people, too. Everybody else got down okay." He stared into nowhere. "Everybody except Barney, that is. Barney's gone."

"I'm sorry, I didn't know."

"It was his last op with the Squadron. The AOC was giving him a squadron of his own. I was going to tell him when he got back."

Eleanor realised Adam was close to tears, on the verge of breaking down. She wanted to comfort him, to assuage his pain but there was nothing she could say or do other than to listen.

"Shouldn't have let him go. Should've screened him."

"I'm sure you did what you thought was right, darling."

"No. Should've screened him. As good as killed him..."

Eleanor struggled to retain her composure.

"That's nonsense!"

"I killed him. Just like I killed Bert."

"I don't understand," Eleanor pleaded.

The man had stopped listening, he was in a world of his own: a dark, tormented world.

"Still," he went on, morosely. "Nobody lives forever, what?"

Chapter 29

Sunday 28th November, 1943
St. Paul's Church, Ansham Wolds, Lincolnshire

The Reverend Naismith-Parry's face lit up when he heard the Bentley in the lane and a little later spied Adam Chantrey striding purposefully up the hill. As ever on these occasions when the gallant Wing-Commander escaped from the aerodrome to attend Evensong, he was cutting it fine. Tonight, he had made his appearance with less than five minutes to spare.

"Why, good evening, Wing-Commander." The younger man removed his cap, shook the Rector's hand. He looked pale, haggard and his eyes were bloodshot. Weariness hung about him like a shroud. "My, my. I'm so glad to see you."

"Thank you, sir," Adam muttered. "I'd hoped to be in good time tonight. But something came up. Things always do."

"You're here, now, that's the main thing." The old man clung to his hand, leaned towards him, spoke confidentially. "Eleanor and the children will be coming back to the Rectory after Evensong. Please join us."

Adam's was tempted to plead the call of duty, slip away after the service. However, before he could dissemble the Rector went on.

"There's something I've been meaning to speak to you about."

"Oh, I see."

"A personal matter."

Adam had no idea what the Rector wanted to discuss with him but it would have been discourteous to have refused his hospitality. Disrespectful, and unforgivable, rude.

"In that case, sir," he surrendered, "I shall be delighted to come back to the Rectory."

"Splendid!"

Other worshippers were waiting to be greeted by the Reverend Naismith-Parry. Adam took his cue, passed on into the church. It was dim inside, many of the lamps were turned down low. An austerity measure, or so the Group Captain had reported. Group Captain Alexander was a little under the weather: in his case the onset of a particularly heavy cold rather than the lingering after effects of shamelessly sybaritic over-indulgence at Barney's wake. Adam was beginning to realise that the Old Man - for all his appearance of sturdy good health - did not possess a robust constitution. He suffered from ulcers and frequent bouts of neuralgia, and according to Tom Villiers, he had been briefly hospitalised with pneumonia the previous winter. At the Adjutant's prompting Adam had made so bold as to suggest to his Station Master that rather than attend Evensong, perhaps the wisest thing might be for him to wrap up warmly and have an early night.

'Especially, as I shall be flying the flag, sir.'

The Group Captain had given in and grumpily retired to his quarters.

Adam made his way down to the front pew, feeling foolish and vaguely ashamed of himself. He had no idea how Eleanor would react to his arrival. She had every right to ignore him. Or worse, spurn him. In the event he was mightily relieved when she graced him with a rueful smile as he edged hesitantly onto the pew beside her.

"Are you feeling better now?" She asked, lowly.

Adam waved to Johnny and Emmy sitting beyond their mother, both of whom were craning their necks to get a better view of Uncle Adam.

"Thank you, yes," he grinned, blushing.

Eleanor seemed genuinely pleased to see him.

A good sign.

When he had awoken that morning it was dark, with the curtains drawn in the parlour of the Gatekeeper's Lodge. He was in one of the armchairs. Although the fire in the hearth had grown cold, he was warm beneath several blankets, still fully dressed apart from his shoes. At first he was unsure where he was. For a moment he imagined himself in the front room of the Fulshawe's cottage at Moorehampstead. Where was Helen? Guiltily, realising where he was he had thought of Eleanor. What had he said? What indiscretions had he committed? Locating his shoes he had crept out of the cottage like a thief in the night. There were huge holes in his memories of the previous evening. Had he imposed himself on Eleanor in his drunken stupor? Attempted to force his attentions on her? Or horror of horrors, *actually* forced his unwanted attentions upon her? Had he ruined everything? Hurt her? Forfeited her regard? It was a nightmare, not knowing. And yet Eleanor was smiling at him as if nothing was wrong. As if nothing had changed.

"I was very sorry to hear about Squadron Leader Knight," she said, her voice loud enough to carry across several pews. "Is there any news of him or his crew?"

Adam shrugged. Okay. He had told her about Barney.

"No, I'm afraid not."

"I'm sorry."

"Thank you." Adam settled on the hard, oaken pew. Eleanor reached over and gently squeezed his hand. He glanced sidelong into her face, met her gaze. Whatever had happened had obviously been forgiven and forgotten.

Evensong drifted past him. He was in a daze. Afterwards, he and Eleanor hung back while the other churchgoers filed out. It had come on to rain during the service and Adam picked up Emmy, carried her over the wet ground down to the Rectory. Eleanor followed, unsuccessfully attempting to stop Johnny from jumping in *all* the puddles. Adelaide Naismith-Parry made them welcome while they waited for the Rector to join them.

Presently, the old man bustled in.

"There's a book I'd like to show you, Wing-Commander. A first edition I think you'll be interested in," the Rector declared, leading the younger man towards his study. "Now don't fret, Ellie. I shall bring him back shortly."

Eleanor made an exaggerated show of reluctance to have him taken from her.

"Just make sure it is 'shortly', Simon."

"I promise."

Alone in the privacy of the book-lined study the old man invited his guest to take the battered armchair in front of the heaped, disorderly desk.

The clutter on the top of the desk had not diminished since Adam's first visit to the Rectory two months ago.

"You said you had a personal matter you wished to discuss with me, sir?" Adam reminded him, in no mood to be drawn into an esoteric debate of the kind the Rector had provoked on that first, unforgettable visit to the Rectory.

"Yes," replied the old man, perching on the corner of his desk. "If I may, I shall come straight to the point."

"By all means, sir."

"Ellie means a lot to Adelaide and I. We think the world of her and I'd hate for her to think we've been meddling in her affairs."

So that was what this was about. The Rector was going to deliver a father of the bride type sermon. Adam gritted his teeth, determining that he would hear the old man out in affable, polite silence. Immediately, his expectations were confounded.

"The thing is," the old man prefaced. "Eleanor's father, Professor Merry, has been taken ill. Very ill. In fact he's dying. He probably has only weeks to live. Not unnaturally, Ellie is worrying herself silly. But she's a very stubborn girl. She won't admit she needs help."

Adam nodded, said nothing, feeling immensely mean-spirited for having so badly misjudged the Rector's intentions.

"The point is," the Rector continued, "Professor Merry is being nursed by one of his sisters, Ellie's Aunt Lillian. And unfortunately, Ellie and her Aunt Lillian don't get on. I don't know the history of it.

Family's can be very odd. That's by the by, the thing is Ellie feels she ought to be by her father's side. Except that in the circumstances this is impossible. Even if she could get away from Ansham, there's Johnny and Emmy to think of, and she won't be separated from them. And in any case, I get the distinct impression her Aunt Lillian won't have Ellie involved at all if she has her way."

Adam's brow furrowed.

"Eleanor's not mentioned a word of this to me, sir."

"Ellie has decided she won't burden you with her troubles. Any of them. And as you've probably already discovered, Ellie's a very independently-minded woman. She's made up her mind that you've got enough on your plate as it is."

"I see."

"Ellie will never forgive me if she knows I've been talking about this behind her back."

Although Adam thought the Rector was taking an overly pessimistic view of Eleanor's demonstratively formidable powers of forgiveness, he did not argue.

"I'm sorry, I'm not sure what I can do to help, though?"

"In an ideal world I believe that Eleanor would chose to nurse her father herself here in Ansham Wolds," the Reverend Naismith-Parry remarked, clasping his bony hands on his lap. "Perhaps, as Ellie says, it's impossible. I don't know. I'm an old and not very worldly man. I'm not really a very good judge of what is, and what is not possible. Nor of what strings may or may not be pulled in these situations."

"Ah," Adam murmured, the penny dropping. "Strings. Of course."

"You won't tell Ellie that I've spoken out of turn?"

"No, of course not."

The Rector stood up, stiffly. "We should join the others?"

At the door Adam paused.

"What's all this nonsense about this local ARP Warden fellow spying on Ellie, sir?"

The old man wrestled with his conscience. He had already betrayed one confidence, now he was being asked very directly, to betray a second. Eventually, he concluded that telling the truth was the only option. In for a penny, in for a pound being the relevant axiom. He would brave Eleanor's wrath later.

"The village's Chief ARP Warden is a man called Edward Rowbotham. His family had some feud, or such, with the Graftons. I don't know the details and in any event it would have been many, many years ago. Well before Ellie came on the scene. The long and the short of it is that Ellie has been accused, I suspect most unjustly, of several infractions of the blackout regulations…"

"Oh, I see." Adam was incensed, affronted. He felt the colour rising in his cheeks.

"Anyway," the Rector went on, hurriedly, "the thing is that Ellie has been summoned before the Magistrates in Thurlby next week…"

"What!" Adam demanded, more loudly than he meant.

"Calm down," the old man pleaded.

"It's ridiculous!" The younger man retorted in a

shouted whisper. Adam's fists had clenched into white-knuckled balls.

"I agree entirely."

Adam gritted his teeth, battled to restrain his flashing temper as he tersely recounted last night's near collision with the small man in a tin helmet in the road near Eleanor's cottage. Respecting the old man's sensibilities he neglected to mention he was drunk, that it was around midnight, and that subsequently, he had spent the night at the Gatekeeper's Lodge.

"If I'd known what was going on I'd have settled the little weasel's hash then and there!"

"Promise me you won't go rushing in like a bull in a china shop?"

Adam fought to recover his lost composure.

"No. Of course not, sir. Bull in a china shop was more Bert's style. Bless him."

In the parlour Emmy had gone to sleep on her mother's lap. Eleanor looked up, smiled as the two men came into the room.

"That wasn't long?" She observed, cheerfully.

"You told me to keep it short," the Reverend Naismith-Parry replied, smiling. "So I did, my dear."

Later, Adam drove Eleanor and the children down the lane in the dark. He carried Emmy into the Gatekeeper's Lodge, his feet splashing in the puddles as the rain fell. Eleanor lit a candle.

"Look," he muttered, awkwardly. "I'm dreadfully sorry about last night. I don't actually remember very much. Did I make a complete ass of myself?"

Emmy stirred, he put her down. Eleanor took

the child's hand, met the man's eye.

"No. You were a little bit drunk and you were feeling a bit sorry for yourself, darling," she said. "That's all. Nothing happened. You were a perfect gentleman. So there's nothing to apologise for?"

"Right," he nodded, risking a smile as he vented a huge sigh of relief.

Seeing his spirits rise Eleanor could not resist chiding him for his unwarranted fears, albeit warily.

"Why? Whatever did you think happened last night?"

"That's the thing. Honestly, I can't remember."

"Oh."

"I thought," he explained, pursing his lips in earnest introspection, "that I might have blotted my copybook, so to speak."

"Did you indeed!" Eleanor struggled not to giggle. In the gloom his face was a picture of contrition.

"But I didn't?"

"No, you didn't *blot* your copybook, darling."

"Oh. That's all right then."

Eleanor leaned forward and on tip toes kissed him, her mouth warm and soft, open against his. Had it not been for Emmy tugging at her hand she would have melted into his arms, forgotten herself.

"I should get back," Adam apologised.

"If you must."

The resignation in her voice pierced him to the quick, stirred more guilt. Guilt that mocked his failing resolve as he fled into the night.

Chapter 30

Monday 29th November, 1943
RAF Ansham Wolds, Lincolnshire

The Avro Anson's twin engines idled as Adam braked the Bentley to a halt. He looked across at his acting second-in-command.

"I shall be back tomorrow. Not a word to the Station Master, though. So far as he's concerned Pat and I are on the town. Taking in a show. That's all."

Mac smiled a thin but conspiratorial smile. "And you're visiting a maiden aunt in Croydon, sir."

"That's the ticket."

"Good luck."

Adam clambered out into the drizzle. The Squadron had been stood down soon after first light, the third stand down in a row. Having established that no operation was in the offing he had rung around, and put into effect the piecemeal plan he had hatched last night driving back to the station from Eleanor's cottage. Grabbing his Gladstone bag, a battered and much travelled faithful companion from behind the driver's seat he threw Mac one last look.

"I'll see you tomorrow, then." He hurried across the wet ground, holding his cap on with one hand, his greatcoat tails flapping in the slipstream of the Anson's engines.

"Morning, sir!" Saluted the sergeant at the fuselage door. Adam climbed onboard, headed up to the cockpit where he dropped into the right hand seat.

"God, you look awful!" Exclaimed the pilot, grinning wolfishly beneath the handlebars of his bushy moustache.

"You too, old man!" Adam shouted as Pat Farlane gunned the engines and released the brakes. The Anson lurched forward. He had contacted his old friend at breakfast time and told him he needed to be flown down to London.

'Something's come up. A personal matter,' he had explained, tersely. 'Wouldn't be right for me to borrow a Lanc for a day. It would put the Station Master in a bit of a fix if anybody at Group got wind of it.'

'Personal, eh? Say no more, old chap. Night on the town!' Pat had chuckled enthusiastically. "Count me in! Leave it to me!" His enthusiasm had in no way diminished when Adam filled him in on the true nature of his business in town. 'No problem. There will be plenty of time to take in a show. And to knock back a swift half or two!'

Some forty minutes later the phone having being passed from one section to another at the Air Ministry, Adam had obtained Professor Merry's forwarding address in Wimbledon. Adam had immediately dashed off a priority telegram warning the Prof that he would be paying him a call later in the day.

Pat Farlane hauled the Anson into the air, into thick, impenetrable clouds.

"I thought you and the Prof were daggers drawn, old man?"

"Ancient history!"

"Oh, right you are. Love conquers all, what?"

Adam was not really in the mood for Pat's banter.

"Something like that."

"Enough said. I thought we'd put down at Weybridge. You know, the Vickers Factory. We can park the kite and get a train up to town from there. Wimbledon's on the same line."

"Sounds good to me!" Brooklands, before the war the temple of British motor racing with its great curving banks and long, fast straights was the home of a big Metropolitan Vickers factory. He and Pat would be among old friends when they landed. At three thousand feet the Anson climbed into clear airs. Pat pointed the trainer's nose due south, skimming above the swirling overcast. Over Norfolk they sighted two Lancasters heading east, then, ten minutes later a faraway swarm of black specs rising over the Suffolk coast. The Fortresses and Liberators of the 8th USAAF massing for another big raid. They altered course south-west.

"I don't fancy this daylight lark," Pat remarked. "All this nonsense about a self-defending bomber force. A lot of old tosh! We tried it so we ought to know, what!"

"Absolutely, old man." Every time the Americans flew to Germany the fighters rose in swarms and hacked down heavies in their droves. *C'est magnifique, mais ce n'est pas la guerre.* Magnificent, heroic stuff but not necessarily the best way to wage war. After bloody defeats attacking Schweinfurt and Regensburg in the autumn, the Fighting Eighth had reverted to sniping at the margins of the Third Reich: the ports of north-western Germany, airfields and communications targets in northern France and the Low Countries.

The industrial heartland of Germany remained the exclusive preserve of the Main Force; thus far well in excess of ninety-five percent of all the damage on the ground in Germany was Bomber Command's handiwork. The Lancaster Force alone had spread many times more havoc in the streets of Berlin in the last fortnight, than the 8th Air Force had to date, wrought in the whole of Germany.

"They need fighters capable of escorting them all the way to the target and back," Pat declared, seizing the opportunity to jump onto his soap box. "Until then, they'd be better off joining us in night raids."

Adam had mixed feelings on that score. Neither the B-17 Flying Fortress or the B-24 Liberator, could match half the bomb-lift of Bomber Command's heavies. Their relatively small bomb bays and maximum bomb loads of around two tons was small beer when set against the bomb lift of a Lancaster which could cart up to five tons of bombs to Berlin, and over seven to the Ruhr.

"They won't join us." He decided, thinking out aloud.

If the Americans came to Bomber Command's party it would inevitably be as junior partners clinging to the coat-tails of the Lancaster Force. It was unthinkable. Anybody who seriously believed the Americans were about to start hauling incendiaries to Berlin for the greater glory of the Main Force was living in cloud cuckoo land. The 8th Air Force had not come to England to be a supporting player in the great tragedy of the age. If and when the *Fighting Eighth* eventually went to Berlin it would be on its own terms, in massive strength at a time of its own choosing, and it would be by day not night.

"Well, they bloody well ought to!" Pat asserted, heatedly. "And they better get a move on. If they hang around much longer it'll all be over!"

Adam let this go uncontested.

"Oh, by the way," his pilot shouted, punching his arm. "I think you're being a miserable beggar about what we were talking about before!"

Adam chuckled to himself. Pat had jovially demanded - as a *quid pro quo* for his participation in the day's adventure - the promise of a joyride on one of his Berlin-bound Lancasters. Adam had categorically refused to countenance the idea. Pat was perfectly welcome to fly one of his heavies whenever he wanted - that was normal professional courtesy - but ops were out of the question. Adam had laid down the law since arriving at Ansham Wolds - NO PASSENGERS ON OPS! He could hardly be seen to be breaking his own edict. Besides, he would never forgive himself if Pat went and got himself killed on his account.

"The answer's still NO!"

"Just checking!"

At Waltham Grange Adam had turned a blind eye, indulged Pat more than once. However, during Bert Fulshawe's time in command at Ansham Wolds several passengers had been killed, both on ops and in training accidents. For 388 Squadron passengers had been lucky charms, for 647 Squadron passengers were Jonahs, back luck. Adam was not superstitious – not overly, leastways

– but *his* crews were and a CO was an idiot if he ignored these things. Consequently, he had categorically banished unauthorized personnel first from ops, and then, following the intervention of the previous Senior WAAF, from virtually all flights.

"You'll let me know if you change your mind?"

Adam laughed, Pat was incorrigible.

"Even if I change my mind, the answer will still be NO!"

Chapter 31

Monday 29th November, 1943
London Road, Wimbledon, Surrey

Adam walked from the station. It was getting dark by the time he reached the address the Air Ministry had given him. *The Gables*, was a three-storey town house set back from the road in a secluded crescent. There was old bomb damage in the neighbourhood, rubble-strewn plots overgrown with weeds and brambles where once houses had stood. The facades of a number of buildings were splinter-pitted. The tiles on the roofs of most of the houses were a patchwork of reds and greys, reminding him that the lethal rain of shrapnel from exploded anti-aircraft shells, falling from two or three miles high sometimes killed and injured as many people as the bombing during small raids.

At Brooklands, Pat and he had been welcomed like prodigals returning to the fold. Vickers had offered him the use of a car to get him from Weybridge to Wimbledon. An offer Adam had declined on the grounds that he had already called in enough favours for one day.

'When did you suddenly become such a stiff-necked so and so?' Pat asked him, laughing. 'Where on earth did all these scruples suddenly come from?'

Adam had been unable to explain. Lately, it had become very important to do the right thing.

The train had clanked up the line from Weybridge. He stared out of the grubby window, watching the dank, rainy Surrey countryside rumble past. Outside the world was uniformly grey, dirty and damp. Here and there the signs of bombing marked a town or suburb. In England the worst hit cities outside London were commercial ports like Liverpool and Southampton, and Naval bases like Portsmouth and Plymouth. Of the inland cities, Coventry, Sheffield and Birmingham had all been hard hit but no British town or city had been wrecked from end to end the way Hamburg, Essen, Cologne or a dozen others had been wrecked in Germany. The Luftwaffe's blitz in 1940 and 1941, and subsequent sporadic raiding had caused immense and widespread damage to property and killed tens of thousands of British civilians, but in hindsight, those bombing campaigns bore little comparison to the massive scale of Bomber Command's escalating offensive. Most British cities were knocked about, unkempt from civic neglect hiding behind the mask of wartime austerity, but essentially intact. Intact, still whole. Large areas of London might be ruined but out here in the suburbs the damage was piecemeal, almost inadvertent whereas, in Germany few of the big towns were intact, the hearts of most were burned out, gutted, the rubble of their outer districts repeatedly turned. It was hard to imagine what life must be like for the survivors in the ruins of those cities, where everyday life as most people in England understood it must long ago have completely broken down.

Fading buff coloured tape criss-crossed the windows of *The Gables*. Adam walked up the path to the house. He rang the bell, heard it ringing distantly within. Stepping back he waited, hoping his telegram had preceded him, and wondering what sort of reception awaited him. He was acting off the cuff, jumping in at the deep end. The Prof had every right to send him away with a flea in his ear to ridicule his presumption.

When he had told Mac what he was doing, his second-in-command had reacted phlegmatically, assuaged some of his fears.

'In your place, I think I'd do exactly what you're doing, sir.' The only other option was to do nothing. 'It's one of those situations where there isn't a right or a wrong thing to do. All you can do is what you think is right.'

Now that he was standing on the doorstep of *The Gables* his qualms resurfaced. The door creaked ajar and a thin, grey-haired old lady eyed him suspiciously.

"Good afternoon, I'm Adam Chantrey. I sent a telegram..."

"Yes, I know," snapped the old lady. "It arrived thirty minutes ago."

"Er, good."

"You had better come in, Wing-Commander Chantrey. I'm Charles's sister. Lillian."

"How do you do." Adam followed her inside.

The door slammed shut at his back. A rusty bicycle was propped up in the hall. Lillian scurried ahead of him into a gloomy morning room. The room was cold, musty, and even though a low fire burned in the hearth it had about it an air of stagnation, of slow decay.

"I suppose my niece has sent you here to spy on me?" The old lady frowned, hurling the accusation in his face.

"Er, no. Actually, Eleanor has no idea that I'm here."

"Then what are you doing here?"

Adam felt the heat rising in his cheeks.

"As I was in the vicinity, I thought I'd pay my respects to the Prof," he replied, evenly. "Your nephew David was with me at Boscombe Down, and later at Kelmington..."

"David was a good boy. He had respect for his family."

"I'm sure his still does." Before Lillian could respond he went on. "How is the Prof? Would it be possible to see him?"

"He's not well. He needs his rest."

Adam groaned inwardly, suspecting that there was going to be a scene. He was not leaving until he had seen the Prof. If he had to, he would insist upon it.

"I shall be careful not to tire him out."

"Will you indeed!" Lillian scoffed, looking for offence and greedily, gleefully seizing the opportunity to take it. "Charles is resting. He's not to be disturbed. He's not to be disturbed!"

Adam heard a footfall in the hall.

"Now, now, Lillian," said a frail, firm, familiar voice. Professor Charles St John Merry, grey and drawn, dressed in pyjamas and dressing gown, with an incongruous faded green beret jammed on his head, and scuffed leather slippers on his feet, ambled slowly, painfully into the room. He extended his right hand, smiling.

"You're wasting your time brow-beating this young man, Lillian. Isn't that so, Chantrey?"

"I don't know about that, sir," Adam murmured.

"Lillian. The Wing-Commander and I have things to discuss. A pot of tea would be just the thing."

Lillian glared at her brother.

"I shall shortly have all the time in the world to rest, my dear." His tone was soft, patiently implacable.

Lillian stalked off, muttering to herself, incensed.

"You must forgive her," the Professor said. "She's very protective of me."

"Of course."

"What brings you to the south?" The old man inquired, moving over to an armchair by the hearth and indicating for Adam to sit opposite him. "Your telegram was a little, shall we say, terse?"

Adam gazed into the fire, wringing his hands.

"Before I explain that," he began, hesitantly. "I ought to say that Eleanor has no idea that I'm here. In fact, I only found out about your, er, illness, from a third party, a mutual acquaintance."

"That's just like Ellie."

"The thing is," Adam hurried on, desperate to say what he had to say before the old lady returned and he made a complete fool of himself. "Although, she's not said a word about any of this to me, I know for a fact that she wants to look after you. To nurse you herself. She feels her place is with you. That she ought to take charge, as it were. But there's nothing she can do while you're here and she's in Lincolnshire. She's worrying herself sick about you, sir."

"That's precisely why I kept my illness from her

for so long."

"It's up to you, of course," Adam went on, quickly. "But if you decide to come up to Lincolnshire, I shall make *all* the necessary arrangements. *All* the necessary arrangements, sir."

"I see." Professor Merry shifted in the chair as he digested the weight not so much of what the younger man had said, but the stress he had laid on the word 'all'. A man in Adam Chantrey's position could – albeit by stretching King's Regulations to breaking point – whistle up transportation, escorts literally at the drop of a hat and nobody would bat an eyelid. He hesitated. "Don't you think Ellie has enough on her plate as it is?"

"That's as maybe, sir. But that is *not* the way she sees it."

The old man leaned towards Adam, lowered his voice.

"There's Lillian to be considered?"

"I only know how Eleanor feels about this, sir."

Professor Merry took a deep, hurtful breath, and gathered his wits. His hands trembled when he placed them on the arms of the chair. He seemed at a loss, and for a moment Adam was afraid he was going to shed a tear. Then he laughed a short, gentle laugh.

"Goodness, Ellie would be livid if she knew you were here."

"Possibly, sir," Adam conceded.

Lillian chose this juncture to reappear.

"We can't feed another mouth this evening, you know," she snapped, peevishly. "Not without the ration stamps."

"I've arranged to meet somebody in London," Adam told her, amiably.

"A woman I suppose?"

"Er, no. The chum who flew me down to Brooklands, actually."

Lillian clucked her tongue. The Professor ignored his sister.

"When do you need my decision, Wing-Commander?"

"In the circumstances, as soon as possible," Adam apologized.

The old man's rheumy gaze settled on his visitor's face. His eyes were thoughtful, and briefly, glassy. He sniffed, coughed, looked into the embers of the fire.

"You're certain about Ellie's feelings in the matter?" He asked, very quietly.

"Yes, sir. Completely certain."

The Professor nodded slowly. Lillian looked from the old man to the young man and back again, smelling a rat, sensing a conspiracy.

"What's going on, Charles?"

"Calm down, my dear," the Professor soothed. "There's nothing for you to concern yourself with. It's just that we must have a talk when the Wing-Commander has gone. Now please sit down, it's most off-putting having you standing over us."

The subsequent conversation was stilted, the atmosphere genteelly poisonous. Adam drank his tea, tried very hard to be civil, and seized the earliest opportunity to make his excuses and leave. The old man shambled with him to the door.

"I'm sorry about Lillian. That was unforgivable."

"It's all right, really."

The Professor took his elbow.

"I shall leave the, *all* arrangements to remove me to Ansham Wolds to you then, young man."

Chapter 32

Tuesday 30th November, 1943
RAF Ansham Wolds, Lincolnshire

The Squadron's Lancasters were being readied for a *Goodwood* when Pat Farlane dumped the Anson trainer heavily onto Ansham Wolds' main runway.

"I might have known you'd be implicated somewhere along the line!" Boomed Group Captain Alexander when Adam and his pilot trooped down the steps into the Operations Room. "Have a good time in town?"

"Yes, thank you, sir," Adam acknowledged, avoiding the Old Man's eye.

Pat meanwhile, stumped over to the operations table.

"We took in a bloody good show at the Hammersmith Palais," he reported, hungrily devouring the operations order. It was a rare glimpse of the fruit now forbidden to him, a window onto a world he desperately missed and longed to embrace anew. On the squadrons he was among friends, at home. Up here on the high wold there were no politics. Up here a man's worth was measured by his deeds and the ops eggs painted on the fuselage of his Lanc. The warrior in him scented battle and ached to be back in the thick of things.

One day, he promised himself. *One day.*

The ops order specified maximum fuel. That signified somewhere distant, probably Berlin. Belatedly, Pat remembered his manners, limped over to shake the Station Master's hand.

"This miserable beggar," he complained, indicating Adam. "Won't let me cadge a lift to the Big City!"

"I should think not, you old scoundrel!" Laughed the Group Captain, before he broke off to catch his breath, he coughed, wheezed bronchially, and wiped his lips with a handkerchief.

"Pity about Barney," Pat commiserated in passing. "Cocky little so and so but a chap with his heart in the right place."

"Quite so," Alexander agreed, curtly. He coughed, again.

"Anyway, can't stand here talking shop all day," Pat declared, massaging his handlebars. "I haven't had breakfast yet!"

Adam focussed on the operations order. Normal drill, he concluded. The weather forecast was not good. Conditions for takeoff and landing were likely to be borderline, and ten-tenths cloud over western Germany a racing certainty. The omens were far from propitious.

At mid-day the target was confirmed: WHITEBAIT.

Berlin, again.

The operation was cancelled at three o'clock that afternoon, half-an-hour after the crews had been briefed and with twenty-one fully fuelled and bombed-up Lancasters waited at their dispersals in the gathering dusk. A convoy of fuel bowsers snaked out around the perimeter track to pump the 100-octane out of the tanks of the heavies; armourers set about unloading, defusing and making safe the ninety-five tons of high explosives and incendiaries in their cavernous bomb bays.

Nobody liked it when a raid was cancelled, especially so close to the off. The anti-climax produced a cocktail of emotions; despondency and resignation, anger, frustration and a sense of unspoken debilitating powerlessness. Some men exorcised the anxieties which had built up throughout the day with a stiff drink, or a little horseplay in the Mess. Others were unable to wash it out of their systems, and carried the quiet trauma around with them like a curse.

It was worse for the Squadron's two American guests. Herman Jablonski and Hector Angelis did not know whether to laugh or cry. The two men had arrived shortly after Adam's return to Ansham Wolds. A mixture of forced disappointment and guilty relief played on their faces when he broke the bad news about the cancellation.

The 'special correspondents' syndicated to report on the 'Berlin Blitz' for several American newspapers had been treated like minor royalty from the moment their staff car drew up at the gates.

"Sorry chaps, the op has been scrubbed," Adam apologised, mindful of his "Ps" and "Qs", keen not to repeat the *faux pas* of his previous meeting with the journalists. "Afraid it happens all the time."

Group Captain Alexander took the visitors under his wing, offered to show them the sights, such as they were, of a darkening Ansham Wolds. Jablonski, the bigger, rounder of the two pressmen asked if he could go out and see the Lancasters being unloaded.

"Oh, no! Goodness me, no! That's not a very

good idea," replied the Station Commander, hastily. "Far too dangerous. You never know when the chaps are going to drop a cookie on the deck. It happens quite a lot, you know. Jolly spectacular, believe me!"

Adam took refuge in his office. The two most experienced crews on the order of battle had been Mick Ferris's and his own. Ferris would have taken Angelis, he would have taken Jablonski. The object of the exercise was for the Americans to get back safely so they could spread the gospel of the main aim. Rather unnecessarily, the AOC had rung Group Captain Alexander and stressed how important it was that 'nothing untoward' happened to their 'passengers'.

'He can't be that worried about them, sir,' Adam had retorted. 'Not if he's happy to let the silly sods come with us to the Big City!'

Back in his office he lit a cigarette, concentrated on writing a note for Eleanor. The moonless period was drawing to a close, the next few days were liable to be hectic.

Dear Eleanor,

Please forgive me for not coming in person but things are a tad busy at the moment and I thought you'd want to hear my news without delay.

Yesterday, I had to go down to Brooklands. You know, to do one of these ghastly "Meet the workers" affairs at Vickers with an old chum, Pat Farlane. I thought I had escaped these chores when I was banished from 5 Group last year, but apparently not!

Anyway, that's by the by. While I was down in Weybridge I bumped into some old friends, and the Prof's name came up.

I wish you'd told me he wasn't well. Last night Pat Farlane and I went up to town to catch a show, and on the way I popped in on the Prof to pay my respects (as one does). I'm afraid your Aunt Lillian was distinctly unchuffed to see me. I now know what George felt like when he faced the dragon!

Anyway, the Prof seemed pleased to see me and we had a chinwag about this and that (your Aunt didn't like it at all - I think she felt left out). You mustn't think I'm meddling, but I got the impression the Prof was worried about being a burden to you. I told him I thought he was talking a lot of tosh. Then he gave me the line about how "it was impossible to travel to Lincolnshire". In the heat of the moment I turned around and said something like: "Nonsense!" And told him that if getting up to Ansham Wolds was a problem I'd sort something out. Before I knew it, he'd called my bluff!

So, I've taken the liberty of pulling a few strings and organising a car to bring him up tomorrow.

I hope I haven't put my foot in it. Especially after the other night. One or two of the chaps have let slip that I was in a right old state when I baled out of Barney's wake.

Until we speak again (assuming you will ever want to speak to me again after my

meddling),
   Yours truly (and contritely),
   Adam.

Pulling strings was easy, lying to Eleanor was not.

Everything was set up. The new Senior WAAF was a revelation; she had made available a staff car and a driver without demur, and pointedly asked no questions. Ben had volunteered to take care of the Prof, to fetch and carry for him, and to keep his spirits up on the long journey north. In the event there was an operation tomorrow Peter Tilliard's navigator, Jack Gordon had been recruited to stand in for Ben and navigate O-Orange.

Adam would make his peace with Eleanor later.

[THE END]

Author's End Note

Thank you for reading **The Big City**. I hope you enjoyed it; if not, I am sorry. Either way, I still thank you for giving of your time and attention to read it. Civilisation depends on people like you.

Although all the events depicted in the narrative of **The Big City** are set in a specific place and time the characters in it are the constructs of my own imagination. *Ansham Wolds, Waltham Grange, Kelmington* and *Faldwell* are fictional Bomber Command bases, likewise, *380, 388* and *647 Squadrons* exist only in my head. While *Bawtry Hall* was the Headquarters of No 1 Group, I have made no attempt to accurately depict it, or any members of the command staff posted to it in 1943 and 1944. Moreover, the words and actions attributed to specific officers at Bawtry Hall and elsewhere are *my* words.

One final thought.

A note on jargon. I have been at pains to make **The Big City** accessible to readers who are relatively new to the subject matter and therefore not necessarily wholly conversant with the technologies and contemporary Royal Air Force 'service speak'; while attempting *not* to sacrifice the atmosphere and *reality* of that subject matter for readers who are already immersed in Bomber Command's campaigns. For example, I describe aircraft by employing their designated 'letters' – that is, B-

Baker, or T-Tommy and so on – rather than using the common RAF parlance of referring to an aircraft by its serial number. Likewise, where possible I look to explain technical terms and procedures in layperson's language. Inevitably, this leaves one open to the charge that one is 'dumbing down'; but there are many trade-offs in writing any serious work of fiction, and I sincerely hope I have drawn the line in more or less the right place. However, this is a judgement I leave to you, my reader.

Other Books by James Philip

The Timeline 10/27/62 World

The Timeline 10/27/62 - Main Series

Book 1: Operation Anadyr
Book 2: Love is Strange
Book 3: The Pillars of Hercules
Book 4: Red Dawn
Book 5: The Burning Time
Book 6: Tales of Brave Ulysses
Book 7: A Line in the Sand
Book 8: The Mountains of the Moon
Book 9: All Along the Watchtower
Book 10: Crow on the Cradle
Book 11: 1966 & All That

A standalone Timeline10/27/62 Novel

Football In The Ruins – The World Cup of 1966

Coming in 2018-19

Book12: Only In America
Book 13: Warsaw Concerto

Timeline 10/27/62 - USA

Book 1: Aftermath
Book 2: California Dreaming
Book 3: The Great Society
Book 4: Ask Not of Your Country
Book 5: The American Dream

Timeline 10/27/62 – Australia

Book 1: Cricket on the Beach
Book 2: Operation Manna

Other Series & Books

The Guy Winter Mysteries

Prologue: Winter's Pearl
Book 1: Winter's War
Book 2: Winter's Revenge
Book 3: Winter's Exile
Book 4: Winter's Return
Book 5: Winter's Spy
Book 6: Winter's Nemesis

The Harry Waters Series

Book 1: Islands of No Return
Book 2: Heroes
Book 3: Brothers in Arms

The Frankie Ransom Series

Book 1: A Ransom for Two Roses
Book 2: The Plains of Waterloo
Book 3: The Nantucket Sleighride

The Strangers Bureau Series

Book 1: Interlopers
Book 2: Pictures of Lily

NON-FICTION CRICKET BOOKS

FS Jackson
Lord Hawke

Audio Books of the following Titles are available (or are in production) now

Aftermath
After Midnight
A Ransom for Two Roses
Brothers in Arms
California Dreaming
Heroes
Islands of No Return
Love is Strange
Main Force Country
Operation Anadyr
The Big City
The Cloud Walkers
The Nantucket Sleighride
The Painter
The Pillars of Hercules
The Road to Berlin
The Plains of Waterloo
Until the Night
When Winter Comes
Winter's Exile
Winter's Nemesis
Winter's Pearl
Winter's Return
Winter's Revenge
Winter's Spy
Winter's War

Cricket Books edited by James Philip

The James D. Coldham Series
[Edited by James Philip]

Books

Northamptonshire Cricket: A History [1741-1958]
Lord Harris

Anthologies

Volume 1: Notes & Articles
Volume 2: Monographs No. 1 to 8

Monographs

No. 1 - William Brockwell
No. 2 - German Cricket
No. 3 - Devon Cricket
No. 4 - R.S. Holmes
No. 5 - Collectors & Collecting
No. 6 - Early Cricket Reporters
No. 7 – Northamptonshire
No. 8 - Cricket & Authors

Details of all James Philip's books and forthcoming publications
will be found on his website www.jamesphilip.co.uk

Cover artwork concepts by James Philip
Graphic Design by Beastleigh Web Design